THE FASCINATION
DIARY OF ALAN SAEND

HUSHED FOREST ENTERTAINMENT

More stories from our catalog

Children of Woodvale Series

- ❖ Donovan's Gauntlet
- ❖ Blood and Brotherhood
- ❖ The Arc of Time
- ❖ Whys and Becauses
- ❖ The Bite of Chaos *

Dyn'taren Guard Series

- ❖ The Power of the Name
- ❖ The Eyes of the Small **

Broken Lightning Duology

- ❖ Legend of the Qi Symbol
- ❖ The Curse of Godfall Golden

* *Will be first available in collected volume*
    "The Epiphany of Mark Daley"

** *Coming soon*

Please see www.jonathanvcann.com for orders and inquiries.

THE
FASCINATION DIARY
OF
ALAN SAEND

Jonathan V. Cann

Hushed Forest Entertainment
New York

The Fascination Diary of Alan Saend

ISBN-13: 979-8-9872378-1-6

First Edition

Typeset in Bell MT; titles typeset in Luckiest Guy

If you wanted to pick it up,
this book is for you.

Acknowledgments

The first and foremost thank-yous go to my loved ones: Dad, Meredith, Aunt Cheryl, Ed, Andi, Ace, James, Jonny, and Nathan. And all my friends, too numerous to name. How full my life has become in the last few years. Between all of you, no matter how isolated I may be sometimes, I'm never alone. Thank you for always listening and always welcoming me home.

And I would be remiss not to mention those members of my family who are no longer with us in the visible sense, yet remain by my side always. Nanny, Papa, Cocoa, Madeline, Mom. Your love echoes here, and everywhere I go.

Thank you also to the entire BHSEC community, colleagues and students alike, old and new. You've all shared so much energy and passion with me, and given me new opportunities to be everything I ever dreamed of being: a writer, a mentor, a crazy inventor. I appreciate the room to be myself more than you know, and I can only hope I've given you something equally valuable in return.

Finally—as strange as this may sound to someone who doesn't know me—thank you to Alan, for choosing me, across universes, as the teller of your story. *The Fascination Diary of Alan Saend* came to me in a rapid-fire vision while I was sitting on the end of my father's street, a little slice of a young life that was, in many ways, the opposite of my own. I decided to just sit back and let Alan talk, and the book you're holding now was the result.

Hey, thanks for sitting down with me. So, my name's Alan, and I...I want to tell you about a lightning bulb moment I had when I was a teenager. I think it's—what? No, that's...that's just the phrase that came to me. Yeah, maybe it is two other phrases stuck together. Anyway, I think it's important that I lead up to this from my early life so you'll understand the context—it'll make everything make more sense. See if you can...see if you can figure out where I'm going before I get there, maybe.

CHAPTER 1
GRABBERMAN GLOVES

Okay, so—the very first memory I have is of me and my little sister, Ellen Beth, chasing each other around the living room with pillows from the couch. Ellen Beth bumped into the square table by the front window and a big, blue vase started falling down on her; I heard my mom scream. I ran over and tackled her out of the way just in time. Mom called me her little hero after that—she still does sometimes. And that was how I invented Grabberman.

You see, Grabberman was my superhero secret identity. I came up with the name because I misremembered that I actually grabbed the vase for a couple of years, but technically, I did grab my sister, so it still works. I made a cape out of an old pillowcase and some string, and then eventually, I took an old red T-shirt and drew a G on it—oh, no, I don't mean I forgot this when it just happened. I didn't call the superhero Grabberman at first—I made the shirt with the G much later. I was just "the hero" back then, and I only had the...gloves and the cape, not the shirt.

Yeah, the gloves were the most important part of the costume, because...Grabberman grabbed things with his hands. They were the...the ones my mom used to wash dishes—the yellow ones. See, because I pushed Ellen Beth with my hands, my hands were where my powers were. My mom liked the idea—she pretended to be scared of a big fly that got inside once so I could save her by swatting it—but I didn't really like it when she tried to join in, to be honest. At least it made her let me keep the gloves when she found out I took them.

Anyway, this was all back when we still lived in the trailer. It was way out in the woods, and most of our front lawn was this really steep hill. There wasn't much of a yard behind the trailer, either—just a little bit before the forest I was too scared to go into. So, when Grabberman went out on patrol, it was mostly just against the evil spy, which was Ellen Beth sticking her head around the corner at me. I didn't love it when she tried to play along, either—Grabberman was something I wanted to do on my own—but I did have fun chasing her around the trailer, and she never stayed interested for that long. She'd always cut off the chase when she got bored by jumping into the pool and splashing me away. We had just enough flat space under our bedroom window to put out one of those little plastic pools and fill it up with the garden hose—we used to race toy boats in it. We always stopped whatever we were doing when we heard a car coming around the bend, though. We kept score on how many times we guessed right about whether it was from Massachusetts or had out-of-state plates. There wasn't a lot else going on out there.

Fortunately, that was the last summer we spent in the trailer, because two big things happened in July of 1989—the bottom apartment in my grandparents' house opened up, and my mom and dad decided they were better off as friends than as husband and wife. The house in Berensdale didn't always belong to Nana and Granddad—they bought it from the old owners after they'd already been living there for, like, twenty years—and when the renters in the downstairs apartment went to live in Florida, they immediately tried to get my mom to come move home, but it wasn't really hard to convince her. I don't think either she or my dad really ever liked living in the trailer, but at least my dad got to be away in Boston a lot for his job. Them getting a divorce wasn't even much of a change—I only saw my dad a couple times a month anyway, and he and my mom always said they had much more fun once the pressure of being married was off.

And the only thing that made me sad about moving was that I lost my favorite book.

Anyway, the apartment already had furniture and stuff in it, so we didn't have to rent a truck—oh, uh, the book was called…Diving for Mastodons. It was a photo book about these…divers who found mastodon fossils in a cave in Canada. I didn't realize we left it behind until years later—I thought it was in one of the boxes my mom packed up. I guess I was too distracted making sure I didn't forget my Grabberman costume—what little there was of it at the time.

Anyway, I'd never been to the city before then—Nana and Granddad always drove out to visit us instead. When we all got in my dad's car to leave, my mom was like, "Watch carefully, Alan—this is the route your grandparents have been taking since you were born, except in reverse." So, I watched. I remember we passed a waterfall first, then a pond, then a cemetery, then two pink flamingoes in somebody's yard, and then we came out of the forest and there was a Chinese restaurant in a field where two big roads met, and then, after that, we went back into the trees for a while and passed a garage with a bunch of broken-down cars, then a farm with cows and alpacas, and then we followed a river on Ellen Beth's side that kept getting wider until I could see the city on the other side. To my five-year-old eyes, the buildings looked humongous.

And my mom was like, "Over the bridge!" And right then, it felt like the car started buzzing. I remember getting scared, but my dad said the bridge was supposed to feel that way because it was a metal grate to let the rainwater pass through. My mom told me to look up and the bridge girders distracted me until we were across.

Berensdale's in Vermont—the state line was in the middle of the river—and coming in right near the center of town felt like dropping into another world. I thought, there's so much for me to explore here! The first thing I noticed was that there were a lot of hills—we were going up one to get to Nana and Granddad's house, and I saw another one out the window with a road that led through the shopping district. The buildings looked even bigger up close. We drove for a little while longer and then turned left at a school that was up another hill, but it had a playground with a big, wooden tower and a tire climb not that far from street level.

And I was like, "Mom, can we go there?"

And she said, "Of course we will—that's your new Kindergarten!" And I think I made a sound I can't make anymore, now that my voice changed.

The houses on our street were closer together than any houses I'd ever seen—our nearest neighbor in the trailer was, like, half a mile away. Some of these houses had balconies and yards—a couple even had both. And then, there was this one house with a balcony that had no rails, so you'd just fall off it the second you stepped out the door, or at least that's how it looked. Anyway, our house was number 61, and Nana and Granddad were cleaning out our apartment when we got there, so the front door was open. They waved to us and I remember being shocked that we had to drive over the sidewalk to park in our driveway.

The house was blue, and there were, like, all these decorative rocks and planters my grandparents put out, but the first thing that really got my attention was when I looked the rest of the way down our street. I was like, "Mom, Dad, look! It's a mountain!" I'd only seen mountains in the mural my dad painted on my and Ellen Beth's wall up until then. This real one looked so big, I thought it filled up the whole sky. Granddad had a painting of it inside—he told me its name was Mt. Wallanack.

And right then, Granddad said, "Yep! That's your view every day from now on, kid."

Nana asked me, "Do you want to see your new room, Alan?"

But of course, little-kid me was like, "No, I wanna see the mountain!" And that made everyone laugh.

So, Nana said, "Okay, then, come on—Nana will take you."

And my mom was like, "Up the mountain?!"

And Nana was like, "Nooo, just down the street, where he can see it better." And then, she whispered to me, "And I'll show you the playground at your new school, too."

And I was like, "Yay!" And I ran ahead. Our street was one big curve, so all we had to do was walk back the way we drove in. I climbed up the tires and called out that I made it, but then I went back down to sit with Nana. She picked a spot on the grass outside the playground fence, right under a tree, and we just stayed there for a while, watching the mountain. You could see the shadows of the clouds moving across the trees, but eventually, I also noticed this long, brown line between them—between the trees, not the clouds.

So, I asked Nana, "What's that?"

And she said, "That's a path for mountain climbers."

And I said, "I wanna climb the mountain."

And she said, "Oh, that would make Nana so proud. You'd be the first one in the family ever to do it." Then, she whispered again, and she said, "You know, your granddad always wanted to climb the mountain when he was younger, and he was sad he never got the chance to do it."

And that was intimidating to me as a kid, because my granddad was the strongest person I'd ever met. He fought in World War II. But I decided, right then, that I was going to make that climb happen for him, through me, and I figured, even if I wasn't strong enough to do it, maybe Grabberman could. I would've run back and unpacked my costume right then just to point at the mountain and laugh, but, I mean, I didn't want to leave Nana sitting there, and besides, like I said, I didn't want anyone else joining that game—not even Nana.

CHAPTER 2
HONORIA'S BACKPACK

Anyway, that brings us to Kindergarten, and this is kinda where my real story actually starts. On my first day, Nana gave me a blue tote bag and a bunch of paper and crayons, and Mom made me a peanut butter sandwich. Granddad walked me down the street, and Mom took Ellen Beth in the other direction for daycare on her way to work. She was...assistant editor of the Berensdale Gazette at the time, I think.

Okay. Another name you need to know, starting now, is Jack Toyell. I've spent the majority of my life with him as my down-the-street neighbor. Sometimes he was my best friend, and sometimes he was my worst enemy, but I...guess he was my friend more often? He lived in one of the houses with balconies. We used to play board games on the back one a lot.

I don't really remember meeting Jack—it was more like one day, he'd just been in my Kindergarten group all year.

There were only, I think, fifteen kids in our whole class, so it was…five tables of three. My table was me, Jack, and Honoria.

Jack and Honoria were always closer with each other than they were with me—I think it was because they did preschool together, too—but like I said, Jack and I did get to know each other over time. I was never really friends with Honoria, though. But the important thing about her, to me, was that she had this backpack. It was little, like, half-size. It made me…what I now recognize as self-conscious about my giant tote bag, or at least it looked giant next to her bag, and Jack only ever used to bring a lunchbox that he somehow stuffed all his school supplies into next to his food, which made my bag stick out even more. But…the size of Honoria's backpack wasn't really what I liked about it, it was the texture.

It was…it was all black, and it had what my mom would've called…rhinestone trim? But…the big thing was, it was really shiny, like…some kind of reflective plastic. I really wanted to know what it felt like, so I…started touching it. Every time I talked to Honoria, it was basically just to be able to sit near enough to her that I could, like, dangle my hand down on the inside edge of my seat and reach the backpack. I think it was actually made of some kind of vinyl. It was, like, smooth, but, like…you also stuck to it a little when you ran your finger over it because of, like…skin moisture. Anyway, the point is, I liked it. And, I mean…I know this was the wrong thing to do, because it wasn't mine, but I think I just kinda…found it calming? I was nervous about school when I was that young, and I already said I was the one in my group everyone knew the least, and when they brought in the milk at snack time every day, I was scared of the chocolate milk, because I thought it was poison—milk was supposed to be white, as far as I knew. So…yeah, there was a lot going on, and I found touching Honoria's backpack…relaxing.

Until she caught me, the day before Thanksgiving. I remember that's when it was because we were making hand-turkeys. Honoria got up to go to Mrs. Carlotti's desk to get more paint, and she pushed her chair out at just the right angle so I thought it was blocking me when I reached down, but it wasn't, so the next thing I knew, I'm hearing her shout "Hey!" at me.

And I was like, "What?" And I tried to hide what I was doing, but I'd already yanked my hand away too fast, so it was obvious.

And Honoria was like, "Get out of my backpack, Alan!"

And I said, "I wasn't in your backpack!"

And she said, "Yes, you were! I saw you! Mrs. Carlotti!"

And I said, "No! I promise, I just touched the outside!"

And of course she was like, "Why?" And she definitely didn't look like she believed me.

And, like…I didn't know how to answer, so I just said, "I don't know!"

And then, Jack jumped in like, "Ew, Alan, do you like Honoria?"

And I was like, "No! Really, I just touched her backpack by mistake!"

But of course, Jack kept saying, "You like her!"

And I kept saying, "No!"

And then, Jack, like, shouted, "Alan Saend likes Honoria Lansen!"

And I was like, "Stop it!"

And Honoria was like, "Ew! Alan, you're gross!"

At that point, Mrs. Carlotti came over and asked, "What's going on here?"

And Jack is still being like, "Alan and Honoria, sitting in a tree. K-I-S-S-I-N-G." He was not my best friend in that moment.

So, Honoria said, "Mrs. Carlotti, Alan was touching my backpack?" And I actually remember feeling a little relieved that she sounded doubtful about it, because I thought maybe it meant she at least 5% believed me that I wasn't trying to, like, steal anything from her.

And Mrs. Carlotti said, "Alan, is this true?"

And I said, "No." Except I was looking at the door while I said it because there was no way I could lie to a teacher's face, so I don't think it was very convincing to her.

So, then Mrs. Carlotti was like, "Alan, this is called anti-social behavior. We need to respect each other's personal space."

And I said, "I was!"

And she said, "Good. Then I trust you'll keep doing that."

I didn't talk much for the rest of that day. I think Granddad noticed it when he picked me up, because I was just kinda making sounds when he asked, like, how school was or if we had any homework over the long weekend. But when we got home, Mom and Nana were at the kitchen table with Ellen Beth in the high chair, and right away, Mom asked what was wrong—I guess she could see it on my face—and I just started crying.

The weird thing is that what I most remember is Granddad acting all embarrassed that he couldn't tell. He was, like, making excuses about how emotions weren't his thing, but I always thought he was a really loving person, and he'd only had, like, a three minute walk with me, and I'd been trying to hide how upset I was the whole time, so the first thing I did was beg everyone not to be mad at him. I think Nana thought it was cute, at least.

Anyway, after that, my mom asked me to tell her what happened, and about halfway through my explanation, she, of course, asked the obvious question: "Why did you touch Honoria's backpack?" And I didn't want to tell her. I was holding back. It was just like with Honoria and Jack—there was something I was embarrassed about, but I couldn't exactly say what.

So, what I said was, "I just like it. Everyone makes fun of me for my giant tote bag. She and Jack both have smaller bags." And that was all true! I did get made fun of at least once—there was a day where Jack said I looked like the lunch lady and everyone called me Lunch Lady Alan because of my bag. I guess the lunch lady had a big bag of frozen food she had to move over to the oven or something, and it looked kinda like mine? Again—Jack. Not my best friend yet.

And Nana said, "Oh, that's my fault. I'm sorry, Alan. I shouldn't have given you an old lady bag."

But I said, "No, it's fine! I like it. It's just different from everyone else."

And Mom smiled at me, and leaned down, and said, "I'll tell you what, Alan. First, let's get your mind off this—

tomorrow's Thanksgiving! We're gonna go upstairs and eat a
big dinner at the big table. Did you make us a hand-turkey?"

So, I said, "Yeah." And I took it out.

And then, she made that kind of pretend gasp moms make
and said, "Look at what a good job you did! I'm gonna put
this right up here." She stuck it on the refrigerator under a
magnet shaped like the post office symbol—Granddad used
to be a mailman.

And then, my mom said, "We'll bring it upstairs
tomorrow, and then on Friday, there's gonna be lots of sales.
So, we're gonna walk uptown to Sulley's and pick you out a
nice new backpack. Okay?"

And I said, "Okay." And, like…in my mind, I was
immediately picturing Honoria's backpack, but of course
there was no way I'd have ever asked for it.

And then, my mom said, "Come on, let's get you
unpacked." And that was the end of the conversation.

I spent the rest of that night in my room. That was one of
the nice things about our new house—we all got our own
rooms. Mine was in the back and the window sat right on the
grass, because the hill behind the house was a little steeper
than the foundation, I guess. Sometimes, I'd open the window
up and play with my dolls on the ground out through it.

None of the, like, rooms or spots in that house ever really stopped feeling new to me, even once they were all familiar.

Anyway, that Thanksgiving was nice. Nana made turkey, and stuffing, and peas, and corn on the cob, and she also made pasta with her special sauce for me, because at that point in my life, I didn't really like turkey. Oh, and she made roasted chestnuts for Granddad because he liked having them to start off the Christmas season. Mom made spinach and mushrooms and made me try them, which I hated, but at least trying them once got her to stop asking me to try them again for a couple years. To be honest, I didn't really eat much at holidays in general until I was older. Ellen Beth liked the mushrooms, though. She was the opposite of me—she liked everything.

But the day after Thanksgiving, just like she promised, Mom took me uptown to Sulley's, which was like this giant everything supply store that changed along with the seasons. I'd seen it a bunch of times by then, but I'd never gone in. Nana came, too, and Granddad stayed home with Ellen Beth.

I remember my mom saying, "Huh. Fewer people than I would've expected." And I guess that was because it was Black Friday, though I didn't know that term then. I think it was a lot of people for a store in Berensdale, though. I hardly ever saw as many people in Sulley's at once later as I saw in there on that day. Anyway, the first thing I noticed was that the store smelled very strongly of new shoes. It was kinda nice. And, of course, there actually were rows and rows of new shoes on the first few shelves as we came in. Their bottoms were still all perfect, since they'd never been used.

But, see, here's the thing—my wild fantasy actually came true. The second we made it to the backpack section of the store, I saw Honoria's backpack, or…I mean, another copy of it.

Nana noticed me staring at it right away and she said, "Oh, you like that one, honey? Here, Nana will buy it for you."

And I was like, "No!" And I grabbed her wrist and tried to pull her away. I mean, I couldn't show up to Kindergarten with the same backpack as Honoria. Jack would've never let me hear the end of it!

But then, Nana asked me, "Why? You should have the one you like."

Which made my mom ask, "Which one is it?" And I didn't really answer her, but she followed Nana's eyes and did another fake gasp, and then said, "Alan, it's beautiful. Even I want that backpack!"

But I kept saying, "No, I don't want it."

So, Mom and Nana pulled a couple other backpacks off the wall, and when I obviously wasn't as excited about any of them, Mom said, "Alan, let's just get the one you want."

But I still said, "No."

And then, she asked, "Why are you pretending you don't want it?" And that was so, like…weirdly penetrating that I couldn't answer again, so my mom said, "Alan, let me teach you a life lesson. We only get so much time on this Earth, so we should do the things that make us happy as much as possible. Will having that black backpack make you happy?"

And, like, I couldn't talk…but I nodded.

And then, my mom said, "Okay. Black backpack it is."

I hid behind her and Nana at the checkout—I was just picturing the cashier looking at me funny. I didn't want them to see that I was the kid this backpack was for.

I never even really used it per se. I mean…it was nice to be able to touch it in my room without someone else getting mad at me. But when the time came to go back to school, I just took my tote bag again, and, weirdly, that made me just as embarrassed to walk out into the kitchen as I was to buy the backpack in the store, because my mom probably spent a lot of money on it, and there I was, not using it. I was kinda, like, hoping she'd forget or not notice, but of course, the first thing she said was, "Alan, where's your new backpack?"

So, I said, "I don't want to bring it to school."

And she said, "Why not?"

And what I came up with was, "I don't want it to get all dirty."

And then, Granddad started laughed at the breakfast table, and my mom said, "Oh, Alan. You are such a funny kid." And then, she patted me on the head and was like, "Okay. Whatever makes you happy."

So, the backpack just stayed in my room, but I think I liked it better that way. Jack and Honoria never got to make fun of it, and eventually, my family forgot about it, too, so it was just mine. I actually started keeping my Grabberman costume in it, and I put it behind my bed so no one would mess with it.

CHAPTER 3
MOUNTAIN MARBLE

Okay, let's talk about cub scouts for a minute. Cub scouts wound up being something I did with my dad. I was never very good at it—the other kids were always the ones who won the contests and got the awards and stuff—but my dad and I had fun making the Pinewood Derby cars both years I did it, and I liked the pins I got to wear on my neckerchief. No, they weren't badges, just pins. Everybody got the same ones.

But see, the first time I found out about scouts was one of the times my dad took me uptown for ice cream, the summer after Kindergarten. We used to go to Lemon Tree, where their normal-sized ice cream cone was as big as my head. I usually brought some home to put in the freezer and finish the next day. That day, after we got the ice cream, we walked back down the hill to the bridge we first drove into town on to watch the river over the side. The mountain looked even bigger up close. There was a restaurant right on the riverbank—I always wanted to eat there.

And, like…at first, we were watching for ducks, or maybe boats, but then we saw some people's heads come up out of the water.

"Oh, look at that, Alan! They're scuba divers!" my dad said, but I already knew that, because of Diving for Mastodons. I remember wondering if there were mastodons in our river, but mostly, I was just watching the divers. They were wearing…hats? No, hoods, I guess, so I couldn't really see their faces, but I guess I couldn't see those anyway, because of their masks, so all the hoods did on top of that was block out their hair.

Anyway, they didn't go back down again once they were up—they just started swimming over to the little island under the bridge, and I saw they had a camp set up there, with a truck and a bunch of bags. My dad asked if I wanted to go down and meet them, and even though I was embarrassed to, I said yes, because when was I gonna get another chance to meet real divers?

It turned out they were kids—older kids, who looked almost like adults to me—except for one guy my dad's age. When we walked up, they'd only been out of the water long enough to take half their stuff off.

So, my dad said, "Hello!"

And then, the one adult—who I realize now must've been the dive instructor—said, "Good afternoon. What can I do for you folks?"

And my dad said, "Oh, nothing much. We were just walking by and my son thought you all looked pretty cool." I was hiding behind him at that point—I hid behind the adults in my life a lot.

Then, the instructor said, "Well! In that case, he should think about joining the boy scouts. You wanna be like us someday, little man?" And I basically just nodded, again, without looking up at him, but he still said, "Good! I like your enthusiasm."

My dad had a disposable camera on him, so there are a few pictures of me biting my hand and looking at the ground while all the divers talk and call out to each other around me. You can see the one guy I said hi to in one of them—I was really quiet about it, but he still heard me and said, "Hey." I remember he had really messy hair, which I guess was because it was still wet. I thought he seemed like he was annoyed at me, so I just moved back closer to my dad, but I kept watching him. He took off his...suit really fast. Like, he snapped it inside out over his wrist. I remember thinking I was watching him make something hard look easy.

Anyway…so, later that month, my dad and I went uptown again and stopped in at the town hall to register for cub scouts, which was what came before boy scouts. It probably won't surprise you to find out they didn't take little kids diving—that was just something the older boy scouts did—but like I said, the Pinewood Derby was fun, and it turned out that Jack was in cub scouts, too, so I got to, like, laugh with him about how ultra-serious some of the den leaders were. That was sort of how we actually got to be friends, though we did get in trouble sometimes for talking too much.

But the first thing about cub scouts that really excited me didn't happen until almost a year later, when I found out we were taking a camping trip up Mt. Wallanack. You remember how I said I wanted Grabberman to climb the mountain, right? This was my big chance. So, I packed my gloves and cape way down at the bottom of my tote bag—my dad was bringing most of the supplies in his big duffel bag anyway, so I thought no one was gonna check there.

Climbing the mountain turned out to be really hard. I could see why Granddad never got around to it. My dad had to carry me part of the way—a lot of kids' dads did. Den Leader Bradford told us to watch out for fossils or arrowheads, so we all spent a lot of the trip looking down, but none of us found anything. Jack and I started throwing a stick back and forth at one point, until Den Leader Bradford told us to stop. When we made it to the camp halfway up, we lit a fire and cooked hot dogs, which I thought were pretty disgusting, and then, later, we made s'mores, which were...also kind of disgusting to me. They were too messy. I liked my food to be neat.

But then, after everyone went to bed, and once I heard my dad snoring, I put on my Grabberman costume and snuck out of the tent. There were so many forest sounds—it was weirdly loud—and it was so dark, I couldn't see anything past the rocks at the edge of the camp. Den Leader Bradford had told us to stay near the fire because there might be bears around, so I ran back inside the second I heard, like, a stick snapping somewhere out in the woods, but not before I found this huge, white rock that felt like marble—we'll come back to that in a second. Somehow, I was just brave enough to have Grabberman sit on it for a minute and look out over the camp.

But it was the view from the top of Mt. Wallanack the next day that was really amazing. I could see, like, the church back in town, and that restaurant next to the river...I could almost see my house, even, except there were other houses in the way, but I recognized the big apartment building on the other end of my street—the one without the school. I guess we only needed one day for the return because hiking back down was a lot faster, but I don't remember much of it, because I fell asleep at some point. But before that, when we were at the top, I found a rock that was like a little version of the one I sat on the night before. I still thought it was marble, but when I told my dad that, he said, "Nah, that's a big ol' chunk of quartz." But I still always called it my mountain marble. It just...feels that way in your hand.

I took another rock, too—it wasn't a fossil, but it sort of looked like one. It had a striped pattern on it. That one was a gift for Granddad.

And when we got back, my dad said, "Tom, Alan picked that souvenir out himself, just for you."

And Granddad made a pretend surprise face and said, "For me?"

And I said, "Yeah! Because I knew you wanted to climb the mountain."

So, then he said, "Come here, you!" And he picked me up and let me sit in his lap while he put his glasses on to admire the rock. He told me what all the stripes and different colors meant while I told him about the hike. I felt really close to him that day.

CHAPTER 4
SCIENCE NOW!

Okay, that's enough about scouts for now—we also have to talk about books. I read a lot of books as a third-grader. That was actually when I found out we'd left Diving for Mastodons behind in the trailer, because I asked my mom one day where it was and she said that was what must've happened.

And I said, "So, it's gone forever?" I was heartbroken.

And my mom said, "Oh, Alan, that was a book for little babies—you're a big kid now! But hey, we have to go to the library tomorrow anyway, to return John Jenkins," which was a book in a mystery series I was reading at the time, "so maybe you can look up a new book about mastodons. Does that sound okay?"

And I said "Yeah…." It obviously wasn't exactly what I wanted, but I figured…well…I guess I thought there might be some of the same pictures from Diving for Mastodons in another book. I thought it was probably a pretty famous expedition. They couldn't have just put those pictures in one kids' book.

So, we went to the library, and the first thing I did was go on the black-and-green 80s computer and search "diving for mastodons." I got excited when there were a couple results, but I couldn't seem to get a shelf location.

Then, someone said, "Those are at another library."

And I was like, "What?" And I turned around, and it was Jack, standing behind me, and I guess I said "what" a little too loud, since he scared me, because the librarian shushed me and I had to say I was sorry.

Then, Jack pointed at the screen and was like, "See that little 'I?' It means those books are at a different library—you have to ask the desk to order them for you. Why are you reading about diving for mastodons?" And when I didn't answer right away, he said, "Do you want me to help you?"

And I was like, "No, thanks." And I knew he thought I was weird because I said it so fast and so, like…strained.

Anyway, I just got up after that and started walking around all the shelves like I always did when I was at the library. It was fun. Sometimes, you could find books hidden between other books that were so thin it was hard to see them, or you'd spin around one of the carousel racks and come across a book with a cool cover that was turned toward the wall at first. That's how I found Seaside Jane, which was a book about a girl trying to get a boy to like her on vacation. The cover showed Jane burying him in the sand—uh, his name was Cody—and they both looked, like...cartoon people, but not cartoons. It's hard to explain, but it was a style I liked back then.

Even my mom said, "Oh, that's a cute cover," when I brought it up to her to check out.

And I was like, "Yeah!"

Seaside Jane was actually weirdly disappointing, though. I really wanted Jane to get together with Cody, so the chapters where it almost happened—and then, of course, the one where it...kinda sorta did—were the best ones, but that was only, like, ten pages' worth of the book. The rest of it was just her and her sister doing nothing. They walked around the beach, they argued about what kind of boat they saw out past where the people were swimming, and Jane kept talking about how she had a chance to reinvent herself while she was in a different town, but she never really did it. I felt like I spent the whole time waiting for the story to be about something.

Anyway, the best thing I read in third grade was actually a magazine, not a book, and I only even got to read it by lying. I was in Mr. Kautheiser's class by then, on the second floor—we had a great view of the town out the window—and once a month, we got a delivery of magazines called Science Now! With an exclamation point. The thing was, though, they only gave each class half as many magazines as they had kids, and in April—this was May—I'd been one of the people to get an issue about hot air balloons, but Mr. Kautheiser didn't keep track. So, when he flipped through the May Science Now! in front of the class, and one of the pages had a scientist that…he was wearing…he was dressed like the divers were, except without the tank, I had to read it to find out why. Mr. Kautheiser said the main article was about wind tunnels, so I thought maybe that tunnel also had fake rain blowing through it or something? There was an air line running up to the scientist's nose, so maybe that was why he needed it—so the rain didn't get in there?

Anyway, when Mr. Kautheiser came around to my desk and asked, "Did you get one last time?" I lied and said no.

I didn't read the Science Now! until I got home—I was too afraid that if the wrong person saw me with it, like Jack, they'd rat me out for taking two magazines and I wouldn't get to keep it. But once I had it in my bedroom, I was home free. The article was actually pretty interesting. It turned out the tunnel wasn't filled with fake rain—it was actually

flooded with bubbly water as another way of testing
aerodynamics in car design instead of using wind.
Apparently, the bubbles showed more detail than air. I guess
that's why the engineer needed to be in, like, half diving
gear—because he was underwater half the time.

But, see…when you combine that article with the diving
scouts I was still thinking about—even though my dad and I
had fallen out of cub scouts by then—and, like…the cover
and one of the chapters in Seaside Jane, I started to think that
maybe I was a person who just…really liked the water. And
then, I somehow got the idea that maybe surfing was
something I might like to try. It was certainly more realistic
than, like…mastodon diving. Anyway, that actually led to me
checking some issues of Sports for Kids magazine out from
the library, and that led to Granddad buying me a
subscription for my next birthday. Not every issue had
surfers—and I was always still on the lookout for mastodon
divers, too—but I saved all the ones that did, in my Honoria
backpack. Besides, I liked reading the comics. Some of them
were pretty funny, even though I didn't understand all the
terminology, always. It felt kinda like overhearing my
classmates I didn't know very well, like Ben and Bram,
talking about football games.

I started watching sports on TV sometimes, too—I think the first thing I watched was actually the 1994 Olympics. Granddad always had some kind of sports on anyway, and he was pretty good about letting me pick the ones I liked, though honestly, I liked it better when I was the only one watching. I never would've told him that, though. I didn't want him to think I didn't like spending time with him.

TV was a thing we never had in the trailer, so I watched it a lot. Whenever it wasn't sports, it was mostly cartoons, and…I guess my favorite sports to watch were always the weird ones I'd never heard of, like tobogganing or speed skating, so those was kinda like cartoons, too, in a way. Over time, I started to learn the names of some of the players and recognize them in my magazines, so…then I had someone to root for. The only speed skater I remember now is Apollo Ohno—from Norway, I think—and only because Sports for Kids made a lot of puns out of his name. Speed skating was so fast. When their uniforms were blue, they looked like Sonic the Hedgehog.

Oh, that was another thing! We got video games. When I was in first grade, I got to try a Nintendo at Jack's house—we played Mario 3—and I talked about it so much that my mom surprised me with one for Christmas. There was a game store on the edge of town—walking distance from my house, actually, a little past the school, though I only found out about it later—and that was where she bought it. There was a weird day when Nana and Granddad randomly trapped me in the kitchen to help them make dinner, and I realized that was when my mom snuck it into the house. It came with Super Mario Bros/Duck Hunt, and she also got me Ninja Turtles, which I played more at first, but Mario was really better.

Granddad kind of taught me how to play, and he was very proud of that. He'd say, "Okay, so it looks like you press A to swim, just like you did with the turtle." And he was right! Mario did swim with the same button as the Ninja Turtles. He just swam better.

Mom, however, was helpless, not that she tried to play much. One day, like, a year later, when I was at school, I heard she'd tried playing the Rescue Rangers game I had by then and thought she got really far, only to realize, after way too long, that she was just watching the demo that played if you stayed on the title screen long enough without pushing Start. And Nana never had any interest at all. She hardly ever watched me play, either—she said the lights made her eyes hurt.

I got so many games over the years. My mom didn't like violence, and to be honest, neither did I—I felt bad when people got hurt—but violence against robots was okay, so I ended up playing a lot of Mega Man. Sometimes, Jack came over and played, too, but it was mostly just my thing at that point, which I didn't mind. I filled up whole notebooks with passwords, and sometimes, I'd take a lucky guess and make up a password that skipped me past, like, Heat Man's stage in Mega Man 2.

You know what else I got that Christmas? A surfing calendar. Granddad got that for me, and Mom slapped him as half a joke when I opened it.

Nana, like, shook her head at him and said, "He's too young, Tom!" And Granddad laughed. I didn't think I was too young to be a surfer—I'd just never been to the beach yet—but when I said that, Nana rolled her eyes and Granddad laughed even more.

The only surfer I knew on the calendar from my magazines was Kelly Slater, because…well, I think he was pretty famous at the time, but I remembered the other names and kept a lookout for them in the magazines from then on, too. I never really used the calendar as a calendar, though—I just hung it up on the door of my closet and looked at it sometimes. I had my school planner to keep track of my homework and dates and stuff. I was just never a wall calendar person. Either Mom, Nana, or Granddad always got me a new one every year, but most of them just stayed in the shrink wrap because I liked the surfing calendar better, as a decoration.

The next Christmas, Ellen Beth got the Sega Genesis, so she'd have some games to play, too, and we ended up sharing a lot. So, I guess this was a long way of explaining how I knew who Sonic the Hedgehog was to compare him to the speed skaters…though I guess since I didn't know about Sonic games until later, that must've only been in hindsight, and Granddad wouldn't have understood the reference anyway. But actually, we did watch the Sonic cartoon before we had the games, so…maybe he would have, and maybe I really picked up the comparison from that.

I also used to watch Inspector Gadget, especially before school, but that show I'd turn off whenever anyone walked into the room. The MAD agents were always almost killing Penny in various ways, and I didn't want anyone else to see that. There was also this one episode where they threw Inspector Gadget out into space without an air tank, and…well. Same thing.

CHAPTER 5
NECK MASSAGER

Anyway, the reason I told you about Science Now! was to explain something else that didn't happen until, like, two years later. I was more than halfway through fifth grade by then, because I remember it being spring outside. And that year, my mom got...actually, wait, there's one more thing I have to explain first. This was also the year Jack and I started drawing comics together—we were better friends by then. The comics were about...well, maybe I should just say they featured characters from the video games we were playing, because they never acted like they did in the games. We pretty much just gave them our personalities, or I guess a fusion of them—we even always made them talk in the same voices without noticing—and all they did was throw around the same pop-culture references we always were and get into, like, slapstick. There were a lot of, like...references to shows on Nickelodeon. We made a lot out of that one Rugrats episode where everyone kept calling Bigfoot "Satchmo."

But the one reference Jack kept trying to turn into a joke were the lyrics to the song The Sign. I have no idea who wrote it—Ace of Base? Really? That's a funny coincidence. I'll explain later. Anyway, Jack thought The Sign was really funny, or that it…could be really funny, I guess, if he changed the lyrics the right way. He was always flinging versions of it around—"I saw your lunch, a gross bologna sandwich not fit to munch," stuff like that. Someone once told me he workshopped those lines in his room at night. The only version that really caught on was one he did by the puddle corner at recess—that was a spot by the bottom of the retaining wall that separated the school hill from the playground, where a bunch of rainwater gathered every time it rained. I was in the overlook corner at the time, the spot across from the puddle corner where you had the best view of Mt. Wallanack, right above where Nana and I sat my first day in town. Those two places felt a whole world away from each other to a kid despite probably only being ten feet apart—it was a small playground. But the point is, I wasn't paying attention to the puddle corner, so all I heard was Jack making a weird slurping sound at first.

I went over to him and asked, "What are you guys doing?" I was talking to Jack, but he was with a group—Ben, Bram, Aloysius, and Walter. Not Honoria—the girls were playing separately from the boys by then. But when I asked, Jack just sang his song again at me. Not to me—at me.

"I saw your mom, she opened up her shirt and said 'come on.'" And then the slurping noises. I think I made a confused face because the other kids started laughing. But I wasn't really confused—I was embarrassed. I knew by then what was inside a woman's shirt, and there was Jack slurping at my mom's chest on the playground. He kept trying to get that version of the song into our comics, and I only said yes once, when he wore me down. I think he used it more in the comics he made at home without me, though. The ones I made at home without him were about Grabberman.

Anyway, back to the story. Sometime in the spring of fifth grade, my mom got a neck massager. It was this red, plastic...actually, no, it was more like...rubberized foam, I guess, because it was smooth and, like, held its shape, but it was also...squishy when you pressed on it—that was the whole point. Anyway, my mom brought this red...thing home one day, and it looked like two fist-sized humps with a little...valley between them, and a flat base so you could put it on a pillow or a chair. You were supposed to lie on it or lean back against it with your neck to massage yourself.

The first time I saw her using it was at the kitchen table, and she made this exaggerated moaning sound that made me feel like I'd walked in on something private. Ellen Beth loved it—it made her laugh—so my mom kept doing it just to amuse her. Then, Nana said she wanted to try the massager, too, but I left before I heard what she sounded like. Hearing what my mom sounded like was already too much for me.

But, see, there was someone else who wanted to try the massager—me. I mean, if it felt that good, why not? I just didn't want to try it when anyone else was around. Or, ask. Or, want anyone to know. So, I waited for an opportunity, which I got one day when Mom and Nana had to go to some girl scouts thing for Ellen Beth, and Granddad said he was gonna stay in the upstairs apartment all night because his back was sore.

So, I went into my mom's room and found the massager on the nightstand, and then I took it into my room. My mattress had a valley in the middle—Mom said it was from me jumping on the bed all the time when I was little—so I put out both my pillows sideways to make a smoother surface and laid down on top of them with the massager under my neck. I felt…something, but not like the intense relief my mom seemed to feel. And then, I...I guess I thought about how when I had headaches, they were mostly in the front? So, I flipped around and tried it on my forehead.

And then, I...I started thinking about something we were reading in health class. And then, I thought about Jack singing that song—obviously not about my mom, but, like...the end part. And then, I...suddenly, I really wanted to read Science Now! So, I did.

And then...something happened.

And then, I was like, "You can really simulate...," that, can, you? But then, I found out that apparently, you could. It worked...differently than I thought it would.

Anyway, my mom never saw the massager again after that night. Lucky for me, she just thought she lost it, or that Nana accidentally threw it out. I hid that thing very well.

No, it did not go in the backpack.

CHAPTER 6
SMOKING PANTS

Uh, okay, so, the summer after fifth grade was one of my best summers ever. It was the first time my family ever went to both a zoo and a water park. After the zoo trip, Ellen Beth and I made our own zoo with dolls in the backyard. We, like, put Blue Hat Bear behind the split trunk of the tree at the bottom of the hill behind the house and stuck an old baby gate in front of him like a cage. I also made up a card game that was also…somehow, a board game? Nana played it with me and Ellen Beth a lot; Jack never even wanted to try. It was nice that Nana never got bored with us.

But that fall, middle school was coming. I was very aware of it because we had this big graduation "clap out" ceremony at the end of fifth grade, to celebrate us moving on to a bigger school. No more walks down the street with Granddad—I was gonna have to start taking a bus. Besides,

Granddad had to walk Ellen Beth to second grade then—it was her turn.

I'd never been in the middle school's part of town alone before—I had no reason to be. My world stopped at downtown Berensdale for shopping and then picked up again much farther away, at wherever Granddad would drive us to. I really had no sense of how the various streets in town connected at that age. The big drop down the hill when you crossed the avenue at the end of my street was like a portal to another universe.

So, just like with the mountain, I sent Grabberman out to explore.

That was the other thing I made that summer: Grabberman's final costume, with the name and the red shirt with the G on it. I had to upgrade to bigger shorts and a new pillowcase, but at least the gloves still fit. In fact, they actually fit better by then, since my hands were bigger.

Anyway, I took Grabberman out into the street one night after dinner. I snuck out my bedroom window and went around the side of the house, and then, I immediately realized someone might see me, so I tried to jump from shadow to shadow instead of running under the street lamps. I hid under the balcony with no railing for a minute while I tried to figure out which way I had to go at the intersection by what had just become my old school.

My mission was to find the evil at the middle school, which I guess meant…go there and check the place out. I don't know. All I had were vague ideas or feelings. I just knew there was something out there waiting for me, and half the adventure was gonna be finding it.

One other thing I added to the Grabberman costume were these yellow-and-black water shoes I got from the water park. Did I forget to tell you about that? It was fun. I found out I really like water slides—there were some you went down on your back and some you went down in an inner tube. There were people dressed like surfers waiting at the bottom of each one, which…reminded me that I still wanted to learn to surf. I was hoping there'd be a wave pool at the park, but no.

Anyway, those shoes were meant for water, so I found out that when you wear them on land, you make these really loud slapping sounds with every step. Running down the hill, I went, like crack-crack-crack-crack-crack-crack-crack-crack-crack-crack, and it echoed off…something. I don't know what it echoed off of, actually. The street going that way passes over top of this big, loud river in the middle of a ravine, and I realized after about a block that it was actually the wrong way from where I wanted to go, but when I was coming back, I looked down and noticed the encampment. There were a bunch of homeless people living in tents on the riverbank, or, actually, right above it, on, like, a rock shelf just before the rest of the hill dropped off. I...realize now that this is stupid, but I thought one of them looked about my age, and he had on these giant boots, and I realized he was walking into the river to do some night fishing. I watched him over the guard rail on the road for a minute, until he looked up and said, "Nice costume." And then I got scared and ran. I heard him laughing behind me.

I guess I should explain the actual way you get to the school. You had to follow the avenue both sides of my street emptied into very slightly uphill. I knew I had to keep the mountain behind me, but it was too dark to see it, so it was a good thing I brought a map to follow, which was also part of the adventure. That's what stopped me from going the wrong way, once I figured out how to read it.

Passing by all these places I usually just saw from the car was weird. There was the deli where Granddad bought his sandwiches, and then on my left was the front entrance of my old school the teachers used, way up a bunch of stairs with a stone wall taller than me. After that were a bunch of houses with apartments like the one Jack lived in, and then there was the store where we got our cable so we could watch sports and cartoons—all of it was closed. There were a lot of cricket sounds, and spider webs were over whatever outside lamps were still on, and water was dripping off of people's air conditioners…it was just so quiet. There were almost no cars at all, anywhere. And you know how everything looks bigger, or closer, when you're the only one there to see it? Or maybe that's just me. What I'm saying is, everything looked bigger and closer on that walk than it usually did.

So, after that was a diner where Mom took me and Ellen Beth to breakfast sometimes on weekends, and then I walked past the game store where Mom bought me the Nintendo, which I knew was there by then. Then, there was a car dealership, and I remember thinking that all the cars looked really dusty for some reason. After that, it was mostly the hospital, which had a bunch of buildings and other doctor's offices kind of scattered around on both sides of the road. The only things past that were the drive-thru restaurants and the big Mountainside Hotel where tourists came to stay in the fall and winter, for either leaves or skiing—those are the big Vermont vacation activities. All that stuff is set up right near the highway exits, so they can catch the tourists as soon as they get off, and it was weird for it to be so empty that I could hear the traffic lights clicking when they changed. But if you take the last left before the highway, you go through the neighborhood that leads to the school.

The middle school and the high school were together, and you actually pass the high school first, so I was just, like...wow, it's huge. I couldn't really see anything because the lights were out inside, and I didn't actually find the front door to the middle school that night because I never figured out the right way around the high school building. All my options were alleys that looked way too dark. Then, I heard something bang or rattle nearby, and then a dog started barking somewhere close, so I ran away and didn't stop until I was back on the street with the touristy stuff. After that, I just...walked home.

But I guess it wasn't as late as I thought it was by then, because when I went around the bend of my street, I heard Jack's voice saying, "Alan?" right next to me, and it scared me so much. It turned out he was at the end of his driveway taking out the garbage.

I, like, jumped away and hid my hands behind my back and said, "Hi. Jack."

And he was like, "What are you doing?"

And I was like, "Nothing."

And then, he pointed at me and asked, "Are you playing superhero?"

So, I said, "Yeah, I guess, but I'm done now."

And then, he was like, "Next time, can I join you?"

And of course I said, "Sure." So, over the rest of that summer, Jack and I went out at night a couple times as Grabberman and the Garbage Collector—he pushed holes through a garbage bag and wore it like a shirt. I think his thing was that he could figure out clues based on other people's trash. We solved mysteries, like where the trail of a black stain on the sidewalk led, or who left flowers at one of the 1776 graves in the cemetery on the cliff behind our houses, or...what all the murals that suddenly appeared in town after the Fourth of July meant, but it turned out they were just part of an art festival. I didn't tell him I was Grabberman, though. I couldn't come up with a fake name— when he asked about the G, I just told him it was my middle initial, which it wasn't, but he didn't know that. And I didn't want to wear the gloves around him, either, so the whole thing was kind of pointless. I really did it just to make him happy and...I guess...to make it less embarrassing that he saw me by putting across an alternate version of what I was doing that made it more into what Jack thought it was.

Anyway, I didn't actually wind up seeing the front of the middle school until we got off the bus on the first day. My street was one of the last stops, so it was always hard for us to get good seats because there was already so many kids on board, but at least it was a short trip, and Jack usually sat next to me then.

The school was still big—like, once I saw it in daylight, I realized there were buildings for the middle school, high school, and a career training center, so you could, like, prepare for your whole life at once there. And around the right side, there was…I guess a maintenance road going from the middle school to the high school, and there was also a huge track with bleachers and a football field on the grass in the middle. There were always a few adults running on the track first thing in the morning. And behind all that was the mountain, just…standing tall over everything. It was really pretty.

But I tell you about the alley—the, uh, maintenance road—because one of the first things I saw on my first day of sixth grade was this guy…smoking there. He was leaning on the wall, with one of his feet kicked up behind him, and, like…the sun was shining off his knee. You see, he was wearing these pants. They were black and shiny, sort of like the bottom half of a surfing outfit, or, a…a diving outfit. Actually, I thought at first that they might've been made out of the same material as my Honoria backpack. I didn't even know they made pants like that. And this guy was just standing there, dressed differently than everyone else and smoking. I thought that was so cool.

I started to walk over because I wanted to talk to him— just, like...say hi, and maybe find out his name—but then Jack grabbed me and said, "Alan!"

And I was like, "What?!" And the smoking guy heard us, but he only looked our way for a second, thank God.

And Jack was like, "What are you doing?"

And I...made up a lie real quick and said, "I just want to go look at the mountain, on the track."

And Jack was like, "Don't you see that guy over there? That's a punk. You can't go near a punk. They beat up kids like us."

So, I was like, "Oh, wow. I...I didn't see him. Thanks."

And Jack was like, "You have to be more careful. Come on, we're gonna miss orientation."

So, I let Jack drag me inside because I didn't want to get in trouble, but no matter what he said, I still wanted to meet that kid. I didn't want to decide he was bad just based on appearance. Plus, I had so many questions for him, like, what's a punk? What do punks do? Where did you get the outfit to dress like one? The only place I could think of was Candle Wick—one of the only stores downtown I'd never been in, but I was pretty sure it was a clothing store, especially since they'd just put out a front window display of, like, fall sweaters and jackets. But mostly, I wanted to meet the punk because...he just seemed so confident. I thought...maybe I could be more like him. I thought it might be a good idea to surround myself with confident people. That's not so strange, is it?

CHAPTER 7
GAME BOY FLOAT

Anyway, not much really happened in sixth grade. I got over the excitement of being in a new building pretty quickly, and I never had time to check farther down the halls where the building switched over from the middle school to the high school, and there were hall monitors to stop you from doing that anyway. Exploring wasn't exactly encouraged.

Jack and I kinda grew apart a little that year. Whenever I'd try to get him to work on our comic—we were drawing one by then where we were trading off every panel and trying to keep following each other up—he was always busy playing cards with someone else at our lunch table, or making up long stories to sing on the bus as songs with every other kid except me. Jack was popular, and when I think about it, he always did have the ability to get a crowd around him for whatever he was doing in elementary school, too, like those Sign songs, so middle school was just a step up from that, at least for him. I only kept sitting near him all the time because I didn't have anywhere else to go. Sixth grade was when a bunch of kids from all the elementary schools in the area met up, so I thought maybe I'd make some new friends, but everyone really just stuck to the people they already knew from childhood, which meant I was forced to do the same thing. I might not have minded if Jack didn't monopolize every conversation, or if he, like, made room for me to contribute. I didn't really feel like he needed me as much as I needed him, and it was awkward.

Every day, when I came in, I tried looking for that punk again, but I usually didn't see him—maybe once out of every three weeks. He wasn't always wearing those pants, but I wanted to talk to him the most when he did. I could never get a chance, though, because Jack would've seen anything I did at that time of the morning, since we got off the bus together. That was the one time I didn't want him paying attention to me.

Anyway, at the end of that year, my mom, Nana, and Granddad surprised us with a vacation to Maine. Granddad had a cabin up there that he got when he was young as part of the G.I. Bill. He actually used to live in it—Maine was where he met Nana. They only moved down to Berensdale once they got married and wanted to start a family, because the schools were better. He usually rented the cabin out in the summer to help pay for our house, but I heard him say the mortgage was finally paid off that year, and he wanted to celebrate, so we were gonna take our first-ever family trip there.

There were extra bedrooms and bunk beds—which I was excited about, because I'd never slept in a bunk bed—so my mom said Ellen Beth could invite her friend Paige. And then, she asked, "Alan, would you like to invite Jack?"

So, of course, I said yes, even though I was kind of afraid he'd say no at first, but when I actually went over to his house to ask, he said, "Oh, sure! I'd love to go." My mom told me to run over right away and ask so we'd get it settled early and let his family start planning, so it's not like I had to be nervous for long.

After that, I got excited for the trip, because I realized it would be the first time all year I'd have Jack to myself, with no one else to distract him from the stuff we liked to do. I packed our comic and a bunch of extra paper, and we actually got to hang out once before the trip, because my mom sent me uptown with money to buy everyone some pool floats— she said the cabin was right on the water. We went to Sulley's for them. I met Jack there, and when we went in, the store was in summer mode. The whole place smelled like that pool toy plastic, and there were blown-up floats hanging from the ceiling. If you went on the other side of the store, it smelled more like chlorine.

We looked around for a bit, and then Jack tapped me on the shoulder and said, "Whoa, look—that one's a Game Boy!"

I knew what a Game Boy was, but I didn't have one— Jack did. I was happy with my NES. But the Game Boy float was big enough to stretch out on, and I had enough money for it, so I bought it for us, and I got an inner tube with a duck head for Ellen Beth, because she'd said she wanted a duck. They both came deflated in boxes that were... surprisingly heavy. Granddad blew them up when we got home. I remember him making a big show out of it and saying stuff like, "Hoo boy, these lungs ain't what they used to be."

Paige's parents dropped her off while we were having breakfast the morning of the trip, and we stopped at Jack's house to pick him up on the way out. It was long drive—like, four hours. My dad and Granddad had to trade off driving. My mom brought along a little magnetic checkers game, so Jack and I played that until looking at it started to make me feel carsick. After that, I just watched the scenery out the window. There were a lot of pine trees, which Nana said were a big thing in Maine. Meanwhile, Ellen Beth and Paige sat in

the back of the station wagon and pretty much just screamed
a lot and pulled each other's hair the whole way. They were,
like, eight then.

But when we got to the cabin, it was like…going back in
time to the hikes we used to take through the magic forest in
Berensdale, with all the plywood cutouts of fable characters
and animatronic displays you turned on with big, red buttons.
Did I ever talk about that? It was something we did when
Ellen Beth was really little and had to be tied to my wrist
with an elastic leash so she wouldn't get lost. Kinda like a
theme park, except now, I know it was just somebody who
had a big house and a yard that included part of the forest
doing something nice for the neighborhood kids.

Anyway, the sun was, like, lighting my way up the stairs,
and the backyard ran right up to the water—the grass just
stopped at a row of stones. There was another house on a hill
across an inlet next to the road, so our, like, water-yard was
in the shadow of a cliff. It was really cool. There was an
island farther out, and sailboats passed by a lot. The first
night, when I wasn't adjusted enough to the environment yet
to sleep, I went down and sat in the living room and just
watched them go by with their red and green lights.

Me and Jack worked on our comic outside, at the picnic
table by the fire pit. We never did finish it, but we got a lot

further, and we at least decided how it ended. I've always thought about going back to finish it myself, but I think I'd feel bad. Beyond that, we spent a lot of time swimming. Jack kept shoving me off the Game Boy float even though I wanted to stay on—the water was freezing, and there was this gross seaweed on the bottom. And every time I had to get back up, my whole body, like...squeaked on the float, and I kept trying to stop it from making that sound because it embarrassed me for some reason, but if I climbed on too slow or too fast to try and control it, I'd just fall off again. Eventually, I realized I could wear my water shoes to stop the seaweed from touching me, so I only got on or off the float when Jack had his head underwater or wasn't paying attention.

I found out that I really didn't like looking at Jack in the water—he had too much chest hair. And one time, when I went inside to go to the bathroom, he'd left his underwear sitting right in the way of the toilet. I had the thought that I wasn't ready for that. I pushed them over with a rolled-up magazine while I had my head turned away. It was disgusting. Jack and I may have been best friends, but that didn't mean I needed to see him getting dressed, let alone undressed.

And, like, see...there's one thing I didn't tell you. You know how I said I met Jack uptown on the way to Sulley's? It would've made more sense for us to meet up at his house and walk uptown together, right? But the thing is, I told him I had something else to do first, so he'd have to meet me after that. My mom certainly thought I was walking uptown with him, and once I had them both convinced I was somewhere else, I was free to go into Candle Wick. It turned out not to be a punk kind of store—it was more like the Gap, which is where my mom bought me my winter jacket down in Ferrisburg while she was on a business trip. I'd never been to Ferrisburg myself yet then.

Anyway, Candle Wick didn't have pants like that smoking guy's, but they did have leather pants. I, uh...I thought that might be close enough, but I didn't want anyone to see me trying them on, so I just kinda, like...circled the rack from afar, pretending to look at other things. I needed some new shorts, right? They were on sale because the fall stuff was already out, and maybe I needed a new raincoat for fall, too. But eventually, there were no customers in the men's department, and all the employees were off helping the women, so I just power-walked in and grabbed the first pair I could get, then went straight to the changing rooms—I'd plotted a course. Unfortunately, the pants I took were many sizes too big for me, so they were all baggy. It was pretty disappointing, honestly.

I ran them back to the rack and a saleslady came up behind me and said, "Were you having trouble finding a size?" And I, like, jumped up to the ceiling.

I said, "No, no thank you." And then I just left, like, really fast, before she could remember my face. And from there, I went across the street and then around the block before I met up with Jack so it would look like I was coming from someplace else. He never knew, and I didn't want him to. So, I guess Jack didn't need to see me getting dressed or undressed, either.

CHAPTER 8
CRAIG ATRICKS

Anyway, my and Jack's popularity problem continued into seventh grade, and then eighth. We were, like, stuck in this pattern of him doing all the talking and me just being kind of there, and I had no way to really meet other people since it was the same group in all of my classes—not that you could get to know each other in class much anyway—so I just had to take it. Once in the fall of '97, Jack was talking to, like, Ben and Bram about going to Aloysius's birthday party right on top of me, and no one said I could come along. It was my birthday like two weeks before that, and no one even acknowledged it, so I was pretty annoyed.

When we were on our way to the bus at the end of that day, I asked Jack, "How come you never invite me to these parties?"

And he said, "Because you're not really friends with everyone else. Maybe if you made more of an effort."

And I said, "How can I make an effort if you never give me a chance?"

And then, he said, "Look, do you want to come to Wish's party? I can ask." Wish was what they called Aloysius.

And I was like, "Why do you even have to ask? I've known these people since Kindergarten just like you have."

And he said, "Because it's rude not to ask." And I knew he was right—I was being rude—but I was also kinda fed up. Our whole school lives revolved around Jack—he should've been making room for me instead of leaving me behind. If he'd been inviting me to join when he hung out with the other guys more, or even if he'd let them see the stuff we did when it was just us, maybe I'd have had more of a connection to them, and then maybe I'd be getting asked to come to parties without having to push for it.

So, I said, "What's rude is how you all make plans right in front of me and then don't include me. How do you think that makes me feel?"

And then, Jack was like, "Fine, okay, you can come. I'm sure Wish won't mind. Meet me outside my house at 5:00 on Saturday."

So, I did. Jack's mom drove us like we were going to the supermarket north of town. I never knew there was a housing development back there, near the woods on the other side of

the highway—that was where Aloysius lived. It was called
Forest Edge Apartments. They had a big block of mailboxes
up front near the office, and the apartments were all centered
around a courtyard, even though some of their doors faced
different ways. If you lived on the top floor, you had a deck,
and if you lived on the bottom floor, you had a patio. Aloysius
had a patio, and he, Bram, and Ben were already out there
when Jack and I came in.

Aloysius said, "Hey, Jack—oh, and hey, Alan." He was
obviously surprised to see me, and yeah, I was a little mad at
Jack for not telling him. I went and sat in a lawn chair behind
Ben and Bram while Aloysius started whispering with Jack—
again, obviously about me—and I basically stayed there for
the entire party. When I got a piece of cake as they were
passing them around, I said, "Happy birthday, Aloysius." And
I think that was the first time I'd talked all night.

And Aloysius said, "Thanks."

And then, Bram was like, "Man, it is so weird to hear him
called by his full name." But I didn't feel right calling him by
his nickname—I didn't think I knew him well enough. And
then, I was like…if that's the case, then what am I doing
here? Jack was right. I shouldn't have gone.

The other guys all started played cards, and then they
crushed up the red hot candy that was in one of the party

favors and took turns sniffing it up their noses, which made me really uncomfortable, so I just sat there drinking water, because I didn't want to drink the soda. But then…one of the times I went inside to use the bathroom—which was tiny and attached to the kitchen for some reason—when I was on my way back, I noticed someone across the courtyard from the kitchen window. He was hanging up laundry on his porch. I thought he looked familiar, and then I realized he was that punk from school—he lived there, too! So, right then, I had a choice—I could go out the back door again and back to the party and keep sitting alone off to the side for the rest of the night, or I could sneak out the front door instead and finally introduce myself. I went with option two.

I don't know how I walked all the way across the grass without losing my nerve or…tripping or something. I guess because I was so exposed, I had no choice—nothing to hide behind that wouldn't just make me look weird. When I got close, I saw that he wasn't dressed completely like a punk right then—he just had on a T-shirt for a band I didn't recognize and jeans with holes in them, and no shoes. He was hanging up a pair of sweatpants that were probably his mom's.

So, I just walked up and said, "Hi."

And he jumped a little but then he said, "Oh, hi. I think I've seen you at school."

And I said, "Yeah."

And then, he was like, "Cool. What are you doing here?"

And I really did not have a response prepared. So, I just said, "Oh, you know…I'm at my friend's birthday party, over there, but it's not very fun, so I'm just…wandering around." And I pointed back where I'd come from, even though Aloysius's apartment was facing the wrong way, so he couldn't see it.

And he laughed a little and said, "Good effort, but I've got news for you—nothing around here is fun. This place is boring."

And I said, "Oh." And then, he just hung up another pair of pants, and I didn't know what to say for a minute, but eventually I was just like, "I'm Alan." And I stuck out my hand.

He nodded at me and said, "Craig." And he reached through the…dangling pant legs and shook my hand. His hand was really warm, and soft, and….

Well…then, after another minute, he pointed his thumb backwards over his shoulder and said, "Hey, I've gotta go inside now, but good luck finding something fun to do." And then he, like, nodded his way into a smile and said, "It was nice meeting you, Alan."

And I said, "It was nice meeting you, too." But I don't know if he heard me, because he was already sliding the patio door shut.

And, well…after that, I definitely couldn't go back to the party. What if I ran into Craig again around the complex? The ending of that conversation was perfect—I didn't want to change it. But I had no way to call Granddad or my mom without going back into Aloysius's apartment, so I just walked home—it wasn't that far. And I actually ran, like, half the way. I was feeling energetic—probably because I spent all that time at the party sitting down.

Jack was pretty mad at me on Monday. He said, "I don't get it. You beg to be invited, and then you just walk off halfway through the party. What is your problem?"

And I said, "I wasn't having fun. It was obvious that Aloysius didn't want me there."

And Jack said, "Yeah, I told you, because none of those guys know you. Try…talking to them more at lunch or something. You can't expect me to do everything for you."

But of course I didn't talk more to Ben and Bram and Aloysius, partly because after the disaster of that party, I felt more distant from them than ever, but also because I had something more interesting to do then. I spent a couple lunch periods in the library that week, which was an idea I had because I wanted to look at my seventh-grade yearbook but didn't want to wait until I got home—we got yearbooks every year. Eventually, I did go back to the lunch table, but, um…not before I managed to look up Craig. It turned out his last name was Atricks. It took me a while to find him even though his last name started with A, because I went through all the seventh-grade pictures, like, three times before it occurred to me to check the eighth-grade ones—he was a year older than me. Well, only, like, five months older, really, but that was still enough to put him in the next grade up. It made sense when I thought about how tall he was. They tried to hide his shaggy hair in the picture by combing it back, but it didn't really work, and you could obviously still see his shirt with a giant skull on it, and also his studded necklace, or…maybe it was a collar.

So, that's how I met Craig Atricks. Craig Atricks. It was a nice name. Kind of musical.

CHAPTER 9
FRIENDSHIP BRACELET

I thought I might get to see Craig more around school after I introduced myself to him, but it didn't really happen right away. Eventually, I figured out that it was because the schedules for different grades ran different—the sixth-through eighth-grade lunch was at an earlier time than the ninth through twelfth grade lunches, and there was more than one of those. So, my best chance was really still in the morning, but of course I could never do more than wave on my way in sometimes if I saw him smoking on the access road and Jack wasn't, like, right on top of me. I mean, don't get me wrong—I enjoyed that. He'd, like, nod at me, and some days, he'd wave back like he was saluting, but it's not like I could walk over there and talk to him when Jack and Bram and Ben and everyone else was right there. So, just…knowing Craig and making him part of my morning routine had to be enough, at least then.

I mean, there were one or two times I ran into him a little more. Like, one time in ninth grade, I was sick, so I was waiting in the office for Granddad to come pick me up after I saw the nurse, and Craig walked in and got back a baseball cap from one of the secretaries—I guess someone confiscated it. When he turned around to walk out and saw me, he said, "Oh, hey."

And I was like, "Hi."

And he asked me, "Are you okay?"

And I said, "No, I'm sick. I'm waiting for my grandpa to come get me."

And then, he was like, "Aw, feel better."

And I said, "Thanks." And somehow, that made me sit up straighter, because for that one moment, I didn't feel quite as sick, which was good, because I was scared of throwing up on him or something. Sitting down while he was standing up, that was also the first time I noticed his shoes—well, boots, really. They were these really tall, black boots with complicated laces. I thought those were probably better in the snow than the brown ones with the green…corrugated rubber toes my mom got me that winter.

So, it was just little things like that for a while. I thought of him as my first new friend—finally—and I always wished we could talk more. I wanted to know more about him, and I thought…maybe he could take me on adventures, like, skipping class and stuff, though every time I imagined doing that, I was scared of getting in trouble. But then, when I was a sophomore, I got a study hall that lined up with the juniors' lunch period, and I knew exactly where to find Craig—in the alley, having a cigarette. It took me, like, five days to catch him out there, but when I opened the side door and…there he was…I almost just ducked back inside, especially because he was wearing The Pants that day, which was extra-lucky for me, but he'd already looked up and saw me, and plus, I couldn't just let a chance like that slip away, right?

So, I said, "Oh, hi! I…didn't think anyone would be out here."

And he said, "No one usually is." And then, he, like, looked me up and down and pointed his cigarette at me and said, "Alan, right?"

And I was like, "Yeah!" I was really happy he remembered my name.

And then, he said, "You were the one who came by my house after a party a couple years ago."

And I said, "During a party, actually. A party I never wanted to be at." "Never" was a lie, of course, but I only felt bad for a second. I mean, I shouldn't have wanted to be there.

Anyway, he thought that was funny. He laughed and said, "Good job leaving, then." And then, he sort of tilted his head at a blank space on the wall next to him and said, "Come stand with me."

And I said, "Okay." And I did.

We didn't talk more right away—he just kept smoking, and I kinda switched between staring out at the field, or at the mountain, and, like…taking looks down at his pants. I realized they were…different pants than the ones I first saw him in, and that made sense, because of course we were all getting taller over the years, so his original pair probably didn't fit him anymore, but the ones he had on were very similar. They just had an orange stripe sewn into the leg seams. He also had this cool belt to go with them—it had two rows of metal studs.

Eventually, I said, "Nice pants."

And Craig looked down at me and said, "Thanks."

So, then I asked, "What do they feel like?"

And he said, "Hot."

And I was like, "Yeah."

And I guess my voice must've sounded like…something, because he made this little half-smile and said, "No, I mean like, temperature. You cannot breathe in these pants."

So, I said, "Oh." And I…guess I had momentum, and I didn't want to let this opportunity get away, and I really don't know what I was thinking, because a second later, I was like, "Can I touch them?"

And then, Craig gave me a really big smile and said, "Sure." And he kicked his left leg up on the wall like he had it the first time I ever saw him, and I just leaned down and…touched his knee. And then his thigh. His pants were really, really smooth, and I could tell he was right that he got hot in them.

So, I said, "I think I might like to wear pants like these." Because why not, at that point?

And Craig said, "That'd be pretty funny."

And then, he put his leg down, so I looked up and said, "Why would it be funny?"

And he said, "Because, you're…you know." And he waved his cigarette hand at me. "You. Mr. Wholesome." And I guess I probably did look that way, with my, like, pattern sweaters and chinos.

But then, the strangest thing happened—well, an even stranger thing. I made a kind of smile I didn't even know how to reproduce later, and I said, "Maybe you don't really know me, then." I had no idea where that came from. I had no idea where any of this came from.

Craig seemed to like it, though, because he laughed again and held out his cigarette and said, "Want a drag?"

And I was like, "Uh, okay." And I really did not know how to do it, but when he held his hand out right under my nose, I could smell it, and, like...I didn't want any smoke in my lungs, so when I inhaled, I just held it in my mouth, but like, that cigarette...belonged to Craig, and he...he was...he was being nice. He wanted to share it with me. I really wanted to honor that for him.

I think he was impressed when I didn't choke, because he said "nice" when I breathed out. And then, he took another drag himself and said, "Huh, that's it actually." And then, he stamped out the cigarette on the ground and said, "Come on, let's get back inside. The period's almost over."

So, I said, "Yeah," and I followed him back in through the side door, which I realized he'd propped open with a rock, because he kicked it out of the way while he held the door for me. Good thing, too, because I hadn't even realized that was a one-way door—I'd only been sticking my head out before. If I'd gone all the way out and not found Craig that day, I'd have been trapped out there.

While we were walking, Craig asked, "What grade are you in?"

And I said, "Sophomore."

And he did that…smile-nod again, and said, "Junior." So, when we came back to the main hallway, we were going in two different directions, because the sophomores' lockers and classrooms were in one place and the juniors' lockers and classrooms were in another.

And Craig said, "Well, this is me." And he did that little salute-wave and said, "I'll see you around, Alan."

And I said, "Yeah, see you."

And it turned out, he meant it, because from then on, whenever I passed him in the hallway, he'd nod at me again, and he started waving back more when I waved to him on the way in from the parking lot. Uh, I should say that the high school bus dropped us off on the other side of the building by then, but the alley was flat enough that you could still see him even though he was farther away from that door than he was from the middle school door.

When I got home that day, the first thing my mom asked was, "Alan, why do you smell like smoke?"

And I got really scared for, like, one second, but then, I said, "Oh, uh, my…my friend, Craig, he smokes."

And Granddad was reading the newspaper at the table, but he said, "That's a bad habit for somebody your age."

So, I said, "Well, he's a year older than me."

And then, Nana was like, "Aw, look at you, Alan, making friends with an older man. When'd you get so big?" And I remember Granddad swatting his newspaper at her, which I thought was funny even though I didn't completely understand what it was about at the time.

My mom said, "I've never heard of this Craig before. How'd you meet him?"

And I said, "At lunch." You do not know how hard it was to hold back all these details and also make it seem like I wasn't holding back any details. I just…it felt like this whole thing was only gonna make me happy as long as it wasn't up for too much discussion, you know?

But then my mom said, "Well, you should invite him over! Your friends are always welcome here. He just has to smoke outside."

And I realized I really did want Craig to come over, so I said, "Okay, I'll ask him."

But it actually took me a couple of days. I don't know if there was a pattern to when he spent lunch outside, but if there was, I couldn't figure it out. The next time I found him, he was smoking again, but he wasn't wearing The Pants, so we got to talking about other things.

Well, actually, I just said hi at first, and he just said hey, and then we stood there for, like, a minute before he asked, "So, what do you do for fun?"

And I was like, "Huh?" I actually hadn't heard him. My, like...brain filled up when I was standing with him because I was trying to think of something to say, which made me weirdly inattentive.

But I figured it out when he said, "You know, like, on the weekend, or whenever you're not here. Don't tell me you just do homework."

So, I said, "No, I do more than that. Uh...I guess I mostly play video games, or...hang out with my family."

And Craig said, "Nice. What system?"

So, I said, "NES. And my sister, Ellen Beth, has a Genesis."

And then, Craig said, "I'm jealous. My parents don't let me have any of that stuff."

So, I said, "You should come over and play. With me."

And Craig was like, "Okay, when?"

And, like, he shrugged when he said it, but he was saying yes, so I said, "Uh...Friday?"

And Craig was like, "Cool. Meet me out front."

So...I did. I didn't take the bus that Friday for...obvious reasons, but Craig said they took his pass away the year before that anyway, so it's not like him getting on with me was an option to begin with. Besides, you already know it wasn't that long of a walk. I told myself that Grabberman could do it when I was four years younger—that was actually the first time I'd thought about Grabberman in a while, by the way. I realized it when I was walking home with Craig.

I tried to show him around. I said, "That's the store where my mom got the NES for me for Christmas, and that was my elementary school."

He mostly just nodded and said, "Gotcha," or other things like that. At one point, he told me he'd never been on this side of town before because he didn't know anyone who lived there, and it, like, dawned on me that I'd never seen him with any other friends. I…I don't know, I guess I used to imagine him hanging out in the downtown parking garage with a bunch of other punks or something, but when I thought about it, I'd never even seen another punk. I really had no idea what Craig's life was like—this was my big chance to find out. I was trying to choose my words so carefully, but…not really succeeding. And yet it didn't seem like anything was going wrong.

When we turned onto my street, I said, "My house is up there. I live in the bottom apartment, and my grandparents live in the top one, but they're usually downstairs with my mom and sister during the day. They'll all be glad to meet you, but my mom says you have to smoke outside."

And I only realized the implications of that when the next thing Craig said was, "So, you told her about me."

And I was like, "Uh—yeah. Well, uh, the last time we...hung out, I came home smelling like smoke, and she asked why, so I had to explain that."

And then, Craig was like, "I'm sorry, I didn't mean to get you in trouble." Which was actually really considerate of him!

So, I was like, "No! You didn't. I mean...I don't think my Granddad approves, but it's not like anyone's gonna try to stop you from smoking or something. They just don't want it in the house."

And then, Craig was like, "I almost wish someone would try to stop me. I really should stop. I need to actually care about my health. No one wants to die of cancer at age 20."

And right then, I noticed he seemed...sad, I guess was what I thought at the time, but that didn't really feel like the right word for it. It was just the only word I could think of in the moment.

So, I said, "Yeah, I...really wouldn't want you to die of cancer." And then, I made myself laugh and I was embarrassed because I thought it sounded really fake. I mean, it was fake. I was just trying to make some comic relief.

But Craig said, "Aw." And then, he bumped into me sideways on purpose, and I was like, does he like this? How can he like this? It was so different than what…Jack, I guess, led me to expect about punks, but I guess he only said, like, two things about them, ever.

When we were almost up to my door, Craig said, "And anyway, I don't need to smoke while I'm here. I'm not addicted yet."

And I said, "Good, I'm glad." And then, he did his nod-smile, and I was trying like mad to figure out what it meant by, like, triangulating what moments he did it in, but I couldn't see what they all had in common yet.

Anyway, so, I introduced him to my family, and he looked surprised when Nana hugged him, but then my mom kinda shooed her and Granddad upstairs with her and Ellen Beth so we could have the downstairs apartment to ourselves. We mostly played games the whole night. The Sega was plugged in to start, but he wanted to try the NES, so I switched it to that.

He'd never seen any of the games before, so he asked, "What's a good one to start with?"

And I said, "Probably Mega Man 2. I don't know if it's my favorite, but I was most excited to get it that Christmas," which was Christmas 1992. So, I put it in, and I showed him how you have to blow on the cartridge sometimes to get it started, which he thought was hilarious, and then he played for a while.

Well, at first he asked, "So, how does this work?"

And I said, "Uh, well, you, uh…you just…pick whatever stage you want and start."

And then, he did that head-tilt and said, "Okay."

He chose Heat Man, and I was like, "Ooo, you might regret that as a first stage."

And he said, "Well, you should've warned me. But I bet I can do it."

I'd literally never played games with another person before, except Jack. But, if you're wondering, uh…you see, the reason I was stammering a second ago was…when Craig started up the game was the first time I noticed his bracelet. It, like…reflected the light? Of the TV screen? It was kind of like his pants, except it…obviously wasn't the exact same thing. It looked more…rigid? But not that much more.

So, after he died five times to Heat Man's stage and I'd been staring at it for a while, I asked, "What kind of bracelet is that?"

And he said, "I don't know, actually. It snaps on like a big rubber band. Hurts my arm hair if I'm not careful."

And I said, "I didn't even know they made rubber bands that size."

And Craig said, "I didn't know, either, until I found this at my favorite store in Ferrisburg. It's called Pointed Question."

And then, Craig paused the game—just before he was about to fall into the lava again—and he flipped out his right wrist and asked, "Wanna touch?"

And I was like, "Yeah! Sure." And I did. I touched it. It was…warmer than I expected. Also, smoother? Every rubber band I'd ever touched up until then was a little scratchier, almost like sandpaper except…obviously, not. Not, like, abrasive, just textured. But Craig's bracelet was totally smooth, and it felt like it was…transmitting his body heat. For a second, I, uh…I…I actually wanted to lick it, but of course I couldn't. I wouldn't! I never would. I was kind of disgusted at myself for thinking it. I was like, where did that come from, Alan? What are you doing?

When he pulled his wrist back to unpause the game, Craig did the smile-nod again, so that was another data point for me, and he said, "You like this stuff, don't you?"

And I was like, "Yeah…." But I was kind of slow about saying it.

Then, Craig nodded and said, "Me, too."

And I said, "Cool."

Me, too. Me. Too. The one thing I never expected to
hear. I couldn't have even explained what I liked or how back
then, let alone did I ever expect to share it with anybody else.
But I was! I was sharing. And realizing I was sharing made
me want to share more.

So, I said, "Can I show you something?"

And Craig said, "Sure." And he paused the game again,
and I took him into my room and dug my backpack out from
under the bed. And when Craig saw it, he said, "Nice bag."

And I said, "Thanks, it's my favorite one. That's why I
never bring it out of the house. Here, look."

And I passed it over to him, and he held it up in the air by
the left strap and said, "Oh, this is awesome."

So, I said, "You can try it on if you want."

And he did! He wore it on one shoulder, like I always
imagined I would if I actually wore it out. I wondered if I'd
have made it look as cool as he did.

And I said, "Uh, there's stuff inside! It's where I keep my
collection."

And Craig asked, "Your collection of what?" While he
was already starting to go through it.

And, like I said, I didn't really have the words to express
what it was a collection of, so I just told him, "Stuff I like."

He pulled out the Game Boy float first and asked, "Is this a pool toy?"

So, I said, "Yeah. Well—we actually bought it for a lake, not a pool, or…I actually think it might've been the ocean, or, an…inlet from the ocean. My Granddad owns a cabin up in Maine. We go on vacation there every summer, and sometimes for Christmas in the winter, too. So, I get to blow that up and ride it in the warm weather."

And Craig was like, "Sweet. What do you do with it here?"

And I said, "I blow it up sometimes and sit on it in bed, even though I can only, uh, I can usually only get it blown up halfway. My mattress can be pretty uncomfortable, plus I just…like the sound it makes when I, like, wipe my hand across it."

And Craig said, "Like this?" And he managed to make the squeaking sound without even blowing the float up, though of course it was quieter than it would've been if it had air in it.

And I said, "Yeah! I don't know, I just like it. It makes me feel…relaxed somehow."

And Craig said, "I get that." He got it. I need you to understand—he got it!

Craig kept going through my backpack and taking everything out one by one. He said, "This is pretty," when he got to my mountain marble.

And I said, "Yeah. I found that on a hike with my dad."

And Craig said, "Oh, I didn't meet him. Is he at work?"

And I said, "No, he and my mom got divorced, and now they're best friends. He lives in Boston, but he comes over at least twice a month."

And Craig was like, "That's cool. I wish my parents would get divorced. I feel like a lot of parents are too immature to admit that they'd be better off unmarried."

I had never thought about that before—like, at all. I mean, I knew my family was unique, but...now, I was actually really proud of them? You know? And when I thought about it later, I realized that Craig was trying to tell me something about his family, too, and that made me understand why he looked sad sometimes...I think.

In the moment, it went right over my head, and all I said was, "Oh. Well, maybe they will, then."

And Craig said, "I doubt it." And then, he made it to the bottom of my stack of magazines and found the Science Now!, and he said, "I'm having a hard time seeing how this fits in."

So, I told him, "Turn to page 12." Because that was the page with the water-tunnel scientist.

And he did, and then he…made that nod-smile again and said, "Ah. Yeah, that makes sense." He kept going until he found my gloves at the bottom. "And, finally, we have these. Because of course we have these."

And I said, "Those are my Grabberman gloves! Grabberman was a superhero I invented in fifth grade. Well, actually, I kind of invented him before Kindergarten, because there was this vase that was about to fall on Ellen Beth, but I caught it before she got hurt…wait, no, I didn't catch it, I just pushed her out the way. Huh, have I been remembering that wrong my whole life? Anyway, this was back when we still lived in a trailer, before my parents got divorced, but my dad was away all the time anyway on business…."

I stopped talking because I noticed that Craig was putting the gloves on. He punched the air and made some noises like, "Ya! Ha! Ha!"

And then, he said, "Like that?"

And I said, "Yeah. Well…actually, Grabberman doesn't really punch, he…grabs. Things."

And then, Craig said, "Oh, like this." And then, he grabbed me—my wrist. And the…gloves were transferring his body heat, just like his bracelet, so his hand was really hot. Like, temperature hot.

And I said, "Yeah." And then I said, "I think they actually fit you better than they fit me."

And he said, "Right, that's because my hands are bigger. See?" And he let go of me and held up his palm, and I held up my palm against it, and then my whole hand was hot, but...uh...he was right, his hand was bigger.

Then, he asked, "Where's your bathroom?"

And I said, "Oh, it's right out there, but let me go first?"

And he said, "Sure."

Because I really did have to go to the bathroom. I'd been holding it in the whole time we were playing games because I didn't want to...miss any time with him, but as soon as we stood up, it got impossible to ignore, so I finally had to give in. But when I came back out, I caught this quick glimpse of Craig doing...what I...think was going through my socks and underwear drawer. And I was like, no. I can't possibly be seeing this right, can I? Why would he do that?

So, all I said was, "Bathroom's yours."

And he said, "Cool." He pointed to my bed on the way out of the room and said, "I put your stuff away." And he had— everything was back in my backpack.

So, I said, "Thanks." And I hid the bag back under my bed before he came out.

He stopped in the door and said, "Should we get back to the game?"

And I was like, "Yeah, sure." And that was the rest of our night. He eventually gave up on Heat Man and switched around until he finally beat Flash Man. We didn't even eat anything—he said he had to go when it was getting to be time for dinner.

I walked him out mostly because I didn't want to stop talking to him, and when we got to the door, I said, "Well…okay, get home safe. This was fun. We should do it again sometime."

And he said, "Yeah, totally. In fact—here." And he snapped off his bracelet and handed it to me and said, "Let's let this be our friendship bracelet for now. You can borrow it 'til the next time we hang out, okay?"

And I said, "Sure! Thanks!"

And he did that salute-wave and said, "Have a nice rest of your night, Alan."

And I said, "You, too! Get home safe! Wait, I already said that." And he turned around and walked backwards for a second to laugh, but not, like, at me.

I think either my mom or Nana must've noticed Craig walking away, because they came back downstairs to start dinner, but I went into my room as soon as I shut the front door because I couldn't wait to try on the bracelet. He was right—it was hard to put on without pinching your arm hair. It took me a couple of tries. It was like nothing I'd ever worn before, and I swear it was still warm from him. I laid down on my bed with it, and I...yeah, I did. I licked it. That was, like, the first thing I did. It tasted like blowing up a balloon.

My mom actually knocked on the door right then and asked, "Alan, are you all right? Did you have a good time with your friend?"

And I said, "Yeah, I did! I'm just resting up a little before dinner."

And my mom laughed and said, "I guess all those games wore you out. Just don't fall asleep. We're eating in about 20 minutes." And then, she walked away, thank God.

I thought about washing the bracelet off so Craig wouldn't know I licked it, but I was afraid water or the wrong soap might damage it, so, I just...took it on faith that he wouldn't be able to tell I licked it. But part of me wanted to tell him—I'd already told him so much else. But no, that was too much, so I wouldn't have. I didn't want to mess things up, because loaning me his bracelet meant he didn't just want to hang out again—he wanted to hang out again soon. And I, like, couldn't sleep that night because I was so excited about it.

CHAPTER 10
DIVING FOR MASTODONS

My family got broadband in early 2000—we were some of the first people to get it, actually. I got off the bus one day and found Granddad up on the ladder, brushing ice off the new junction box on the roof.

He shouted down, "This Internet is defeating me, Alan! I need my genius grandson."

So, I said, "Okay," and we spent that whole weekend getting things set up and, like, functional together. I don't know why he was clearing ice—the problem was with his router settings. We'd gotten the computer at Christmas 1997, but I'd never used it much before then except for school, because the games on the Nintendo and Sega were still much better. But after Granddad and I got the Internet running, I realized I could use Yahoo to search for anything, and then, I was like—oh, I can use it to search for anything!

So, that was the first time I ever tried to find a word for what I was, or…what I liked. I think I wanted to be able to talk about it with Craig better. The problem was, searches ran off words, so I was kind of starting without the one thing I needed. And obviously, I couldn't do this with Granddad around, so I snuck back into the upstairs apartment that night after everyone had gone to bed. I just tried searching for, like, some of the things in my collection, plus, like…shiny pants and punks. I got the most results when I tried looking up rubber bracelets, but…honestly, I think the things I saw, I wasn't…ready to see? No, it's more like it was a version of what I liked that I didn't want to see. The words…"bizarre" and "extreme" came up a lot, and I didn't really think I was either of those things. Anyway, I got so embarrassed I couldn't even look at the screen for more than a second at a time. I did try to print one of the pictures out that showed me the closest thing to Craig's pants I'd seen—I wanted to remember what brand they were—but I forgot how loud the printer was, and I panicked and had to unplug both it and the computer before I woke the whole house up. I could still hear Granddad snoring after that, which was kind of amazing.

Anyway, Craig had been over a few times by then, and I saw him at lunch at least once a week at school. We started making plans for it—he'd tell me in the hall when he was gonna be outside during our free period so I could join him. We'd talk about games and classes and stuff, and he'd ask me about my collection, and sometimes, he showed me some of his stuff, too. He had a lot of bracelets. I was sad when I had to give the one he lent me back, but I tried not to show it. I didn't want to make it weird.

He asked me, "Did you feel like a rebel, wearing this all weekend?"

And I said, "Sort of. It was covered by my shirt sleeve most of the time."

And Craig laughed and said, "Of course it was."

But I said, "I liked it though."

And he said, "Of course you did."

And it went on like that for the whole next year. It was really nice to have someone I could be open about this stuff with, and the side alley at school was pretty out of the way, so I was never worried about being overheard. The only problem was Jack—if he saw me, like, turning down the exit hall and went, "Alan, where are you going?" I couldn't get away, because I couldn't explain it. I was always really mad when he made me miss time with Craig like that, and every time it happened, I got afraid that when I went back, Craig wouldn't be there anymore. Thankfully, that's not how it went. Craig seemed to understand that I couldn't always make it, even if I wanted to. His invitations were more like, "Hey, I'm going outside today, if you're free," which was actually pleasantly low-pressure, after I...confirmed enough times that he really wasn't gonna leave me hanging. Him going out for a smoke was something he was gonna do anyway—he just wanted me to join him when I was able.

He eventually stopped smoking, which was good, because I didn't really want to keep doing it, but I also didn't want to say no when he offered to share his cigarettes, because...well, it just felt cool. He was cool, and I wanted to be cool, too, like I said. I realize I'm not exactly the poster child for avoiding peer pressure here, but whatever. The point is, after he stopped smoking, we just stood around and talked.

On my first fishing trip with my dad that season—oh, uh, this was the next spring, when my dad got really into fishing for a while—and I always used to look forward to those trips with him because there was so much to catch him up on. Anyway, on our first trip that year, I guess I must've just talked about Craig for, like, an hour—you know, to a limited degree in terms of the subject matter, like...just about the games we were playing and the music we were listening to and stuff—because eventually, my dad said, "Sounds like you and Craig have gotten to be really close friends this year."

And I was like, "Yeah, I guess we have." And it was nice to feel like it was true.

Actually, a little later on that same trip was when my dad said, "Guess what, kiddo? I finally sold our old trailer." I know this sounds random, but I promise it's important.

So, I was like, "You still had it all this time?"

And he was like, "Well, yeah, nobody wanted to buy it. The trailer's been vacant ever since we left. I cut off the utilities right away, but I was still paying lot fees, so I'll be glad to get out from under that."

And I was like, "Okay, good. I'm happy for you."

When we were on our way home later, and we turned onto my street, my dad did ask, "So, how's Jack? He still living there?" Because we were passing his house.

And I was like, "Yeah. Jack's fine." But really, I thought, who cares about Jack? He never seemed to care about me except as, like, his backup friend. But I guess...in some way, I guess, he was my backup friend, too, because I couldn't spend all day, every day with Craig, thanks to our schedules—plus I didn't want to annoy him—and I still needed somewhere to go in the cafeteria, and people to work with in class and stuff. Besides that, it was, like...easier? No, that's the wrong word, but...once again, I don't really know the right one. I didn't feel like I was sneaking around with Jack—I felt like I was doing what I was supposed to do. And as much as I really liked hanging out with Craig, I was technically sneaking out of school to do it, so there was always this fear in the back of my mind about…getting caught, maybe? And, like, I was still so afraid of Jack knowing. It goes back to that whole "not up for discussion" thing—I had to keep my worlds separate. What I liked felt too, like, volatile at that point for anyone but Craig to understand, and…Craig essentially was what I liked. As soon as anyone saw me with him, it'd be obvious.

That's why I ran away after he got his driver's license, and I'm still so ashamed about that. Me and Jack were walking out of school one day in May, to the bus, and then I heard a car honk and someone shout, "Yo, Alan!" And I turned around, and it was Craig—he was driving his mom's brown Toyota Camry through the alley, which he wasn't actually allowed to do, because the next thing I heard was some teacher going, "Hey!" and walking up to the driver's side window to yell at him, after which I heard Craig go, "I'm sorry, I'm sorry, I'm going right now," and then I heard the gears shift because it was a really old car.

And then, Jack was like, "Alan, why is that older kid yelling at you?"

And I was like, "I don't know?"

And then, Jack was like, "Have you been getting bullied without telling me?" And right as he was saying that, Craig was starting to drive toward us, and when he waved, I could see that he had The Bracelet on, and I was like, Jack can't know, so I just took off running. I ran around the bus, I ran across the lawns across the street from the school and through the yards that didn't have fences—before I made a point of doing that, I almost ran into a fence and had to stop and work my way back around for a minute—until I came back out on one the streets that ran parallel to the highway so I'd be off the bus route.

Craig found me a couple minutes later—he drove after me. I stopped when I heard the car coming up behind me. I must've looked mad or something, because he looked upset, but not in an angry way. It was more like he was...scared? I felt pretty awful about it.

He already had the windows down, so as soon as he pulled up, he could say, "Hey, what was that all about?"

And at first, I just said, "Nothing." I had to look away because he was wearing The Pants, too, on top of The Bracelet, and I felt wrong staring at him right then.

But then Craig asked, "Why did you run away from me? I just got my driver's license—I wanted to pick you up and give you a ride home to celebrate."

So, I told him the truth. I said, "I wasn't running from you, I was running from Jack."

And Craig said, "That's the guy who lives on your street, right?" He reached over to open the passenger side door and was like, "Here, come on, sit," so I got in the car. I kinda couldn't look away when he was stretching out, because his pants got…tighter? It was like the way they kinda…heaved into him when he was walking, and he must've noticed that because he said, "You can touch." Which I did—I put my hand on his knee.

And then, he asked, "So, was Jack being mean to you or something?"

And I said, "No. But he is sometimes, and I…." And I knew, even then, that it was taking me too long to decide what to say, because Craig started looking sad again, so the best I could do fast was to say, "I just didn't want to give him the chance to be mean to you, too, that's all." And that didn't feel like the truth, so I felt guilty when Craig looked like he understood, but…it was like, somehow, even though I couldn't find a way to phrase what I was actually thinking, he figured it out just from that, and he was okay with it.

He said, "Oh, I see. Jack's the kind of friend you have to try to fit in with, isn't he?"

And at first, I said, "No." But then, a second later, I was like, "Well, maybe, sometimes. The thing is, I really don't fit in with him, much less anyone else."

That made Craig laugh, and he said, "Yeah, I know that feeling." He shook my shoulder, which was something he'd never done before—it actually made me shiver. And then, he said, "Come on, let me drive you home. Don't let Jack ruin your day."

And I was like, "Okay." And then, I asked, "You want to come in and keep trying to beat Carmen Sandiego?"

But Craig said, "No, I can't, sorry. My mom needs the car back right away. I could do tomorrow, though."

So, I was like, "Sure! Tomorrow." And so, Craig came over the next day. And between getting out of the car and then, I avoided Jack like the plague. I walked to and from school, I had lunch in the library, because the last thing I needed was for Jack to screw things up again.

Carmen Sandiego was this impossible game my mom got me, like, three birthdays before then, when I think she took Granddad calling me a "genius" too literally. You had to know stuff about history that I don't think classes taught until college. I mean, it was an NES game that came with a book—a mini encyclopedia, actually. You had to chase criminals in a time machine, and if you took too long to find

them, you lost. I'd never even caught one, which Craig took
as a challenge, so we spent that whole afternoon—oh, it was a
Friday, that's important—we spent that whole Friday
afternoon taking turns dog-earing the book and scanning
through it as fast we could looking for the answer to the
questions the game gave us. We came close enough to take a
guess at who the criminal was once, but we guessed wrong,
so we lost anyway.

The rest of my family had started hanging around more
when Craig came over, so they were all getting used to each
other. He liked Nana a lot, and he got pretty good with Ellen
Beth, who was a sixth-grader by then, just like I was the first
time I saw Craig. She was still weird—she liked to, like, draw
cats on Craig's arms, but he always let her. He never wore
The Pants over to my house, or even The Bracelet after that
first time. Actually, he more or less dressed punk-lite in front
of my family, with, like, unripped jeans and band shirts that
didn't have skulls and blood on them, and to be honest, it was
a little disappointing, but on the other hand, I don't know
what I would've done if he was dressed up like that with
everyone else right there watching. It was like he knew that,
or maybe he had his own reasons.

Anyway, when it got to be time for dinner—which my
mom kept inviting Craig to, even though he always said no—

I went to walk him out, and when I opened the door, Jack was standing there about to knock.

And he was like, "There you are! I've been looking for you all day. You were supposed to help with our Cask of Amontillado homework in study hall—where were you?"

And I was like, "Oh, crap, Jack, I'm so sorry." The Cask of Amontillado was a story we were reading in English—we were supposed to write response papers about it, and Jack had asked me to work on that with him. I completely forgot.

So, then Jack was like, "I thought you were sick or something—I was coming to check up on you. I mean, after you ran away yesterday…." And then, he stopped talking for a second and looked at Craig, because we'd both heard him shut my front door behind us, and then, Jack said, "Wait, is this seriously what it looks like? Did you actually blow me off just to beg a punk to hang out with you as part of satisfying your…weird fetishes?"

And that made…my head burn. I was embarrassed he said it, I was embarrassed he knew it, I was embarrassed Craig now knew it when I'd been trying so hard to keep the true depth of my…fascination away from him, and I was terrified Mom, Nana, Granddad, and Ellen Beth might've overheard it.

So, my first instinct was to say, "I—I don't—"

But then, Jack said, "Alan, it's obvious. It's been obvious ever since we were kids and you tried to hide how you were looking for that Diving for Mastodons book in the library. And then, there were all those, like…surfing magazines you used to check out, and pretty much the second we got to middle school, you couldn't stop staring at guys like…him." And he pointed at Craig when he said that, and then, he said, "It wasn't a problem before it started impacting our friendship and our schoolwork, and before it started making you put yourself in…dangerous situations."

So, I was like, "What do you know? And why do you suddenly care? I'm just your backup friend, aren't I? You're only even here right now because you needed me to help you write a paper about a story you didn't read."

And Jack was like, "How are you my backup friend?"

So, I was like, "Come on! You never talk to me at lunch anymore. You never want to…work on our comics or play video games with me or anything. All you do is talk sports with Bram and Ben and hit on Honoria." Which was something else he'd started doing—so much for me being the one who had the hots for her. I finally told him, "All you care about is being popular, and you're not gonna get that through me, so I just wind up as an afterthought."

And then, Jack said, "You mean like I'm your afterthought right now, or whenever you cut study hall to go God-knows-where? Although I guess now, I know where."

And I was like, "Who are you to judge me?!"

And Jack said, "Right now, I'm the ten-year friend you're throwing away for some strange fantasy. Come find me after you take a cold shower." And then, he walked away to go home, and I just stared at him—well, at his back, I guess.

I was really scared to look at Craig when he came up to me, but all he said was, "What's Diving for Mastodons?"

And that was, like, the one thing I wasn't prepared for, so I pretty much tripped over my own tongue for a minute before I said, "It's this book I used to have when I was a kid, but I left it behind in our old trailer, which is abandoned now, so it's gone. I've been trying to find another copy ever since."

And Craig said, "Wait, the trailer's abandoned?"

And I said, "According to my dad, anyway."

And Craig said, "Has it been abandoned since you left?"

And I said, "Yeah, why?"

And Craig did his smile-nod at me and twirled his car keys in his hand and said, "So, let's go get it. Let's go get your book."

And I was like, "Wait, now?"

And Craig was like, "Yeah. No reason we can't right?"

And I said, "Craig, the trailer is, like, half an hour away. It's in Massachusetts."

And Craig said, "Massachusetts isn't that far. Come on, I'm up for an adventure."

And even after everything that happened, it turned out I was up for an adventure, too, plus the idea that I could finally have my book back entranced me, so I went back inside for a second to tell my mom I was eating out—and, thankfully, she did not seem to have overheard anything that went on outside—and then Craig and I spent the next half-hour retracing my family's steps across the bridge out of Berensdale and down through the back roads of New Hampshire into Massachusetts.

A little over halfway there, I said, "Turn left, past that building. It used to be a Chinese restaurant." It looked like it had caught fire at some point in the last ten years—the windows were all boarded up. And after that, I said, "Okay, now the next thing we're looking for is a yard with pink flamingoes. I hope it's still there."

And Craig was like, "How do you remember all this stuff?"

And I said, "Moving to the city was the most important day of my life—of course I remember it. Besides, there was nothing else to look at out here besides landmarks."

And Craig laughed and said, "Alan, Berensdale is not 'the city.'"

And I said, "It's not?"

And he said, "No. Haven't you ever been to Boston?"

And I said, "I haven't even been to Ferrisburg."

And Craig said, "Right, that's something we have to remember to change at some point."

The flamingoes were still there, which was good, even though they weren't as pink after all that time, so I knew where to turn. After that, it was easy, because we were back in the area of my childhood—I'd seen everything there on more than just one day. We followed the cemetery to the pond, then the pond to the waterfall, and then I saw the one road that curved uphill next to a big rock and I said to Craig, "There, turn there." And a minute later, we were back at my trailer…or at least what was left of it.

I don't know if I would've felt different if I'd had more of an attachment to the place—maybe it would've upset me to see it all run-down down and dark, with the roof falling in and Ellen Beth's pool cracked apart like glass from age and the harsh winters, but at the time, I was just like, "Whoa."

And Craig was like, "Yeah, this is cool."

And I was like, "It…surprisingly is."

And Craig was like, "You really lived here?" This was while we were getting out of the car and I was starting to walk up the hill—it was so much steeper than I'd remembered. Erosion, maybe.

So, I said, "Only until I was five."

And Craig was like, "It's so far out in the middle of nowhere."

That got me to laugh, and I said, "Yeah, my mom and dad didn't like it, either, but I think it was all we could afford for a while. And I guess most other people wouldn't like it, either, or else my dad wouldn't have had such a hard time selling the lot. I know I'm much happier where I am now."

And Craig was like, "Me, too." And I think I was so distracted that I didn't parse what he meant until I went back over it in my head later.

The front door was off its hinges, so I could open it without having a key, but it was so stuck that it took me a couple tries. As soon as I got it open, Craig made a choking sound and backed up with his jacket sleeve over his face, because the inside smelled a lot like mold.

He was like, "Oh, God, it's disgusting in there. Do you mind if I wait out here?"

And I said, "Yeah, it's okay. This won't take me long." Because I knew exactly where the book was—on the little shelf between my and Ellen Beth's beds.

There was a baby tree growing in our old bedroom, and the limb of a bigger tree was sticking through a hole in the ceiling. The carpet was squishy and made, like, sucking noises on my way past the living room, so I thought to myself, Craig's right, I shouldn't spend too much time in here or else I'm gonna get sick, and I, like, pulled my shirt up to cover my nose and mouth. And when I finally laid my hands on Diving for Mastodons again for the first time in a decade…I don't know what I expected, but it was so water-damaged, it was unreadable. The pages were, like, black from mold, and you could only make out one picture in the back anymore that wasn't even my favorite one.

When I went back out to show it to Craig, he pulled back and said, "Just, like, hold it up so I can see."

And I said, "There's not much to see, sadly." But I still did it, and he pulled his car flashlight out of his jacket while I told him, "There's really only one picture left."

But he looked for a couple seconds, and then he said, "Wow, though, I see it. This is what started it all, huh? The first item in your collection."

And I was like, "I guess." Is it weird that I'd never thought about it like that before?

At first, I said, "We should probably just leave it here, right?"

But then, Craig said, "No, we came all this way—we might as well take it. Just…." And then, he ran back down to the car and opened the back door, dug around on the floor for a minute, and came back dumping out an old Burger King bag. He said, "Just put it in this okay? Actually…." And then, he went back and got another one. "Maybe two."

Before we got in the car to go home, Craig went behind the trailer to pee, and he brought his backpack with him for some reason. I made a point of not listening—I actually stood on his side of the car and just looked up and down the road as much as I could in the one street light. I remembered how Ellen Beth and I used to listen for cars on that road, and how I didn't know back then what was past the curve in either direction. My front yard was the edge of my world at that age, just like my street in Berensdale was the edge of my world until I became a sixth-grader. I thought about how much smaller all these places seemed after I'd been out more.

But then, Craig came back, and I jumped because he was wearing The Pants, and I said, "You, uh…you changed."

And Craig said, "Yeah, I've been keeping these in my backpack sometimes when we hang out, just in case I wanna do something like...I dunno, cheer you up?"

And I said, "I'm actually fine right now, but thank you." I was shocked.

And then, Craig said, "Good, because when we get back, there's something I want to ask you."

And then, we got in the car and started driving back to Berensdale, and let me tell you, that statement was hanging over my head the entire way. It was a good thing I could focus on listening to the radio. Craig had Ace of Base on, playing Beautiful Life—see, that's why I said it was a funny coincidence about The Sign before, remember? Craig liked dance music, which was surprising at first for a punk, but at some point, I realized I'd never even heard him call himself that, and what did I know about what punks liked, anyway? I only knew one, and it's not like I'd ever gotten around to asking him about his...culture, or whatever. Even with all the stuff we talked about, that was the one topic that never came up. I always seemed to get distracted from it by other things he was telling me, or whatever we were doing. But anyway, back to the drive—there weren't even any other cars on the road that night. It would've been dark enough to see constellations if it wasn't for Craig's headlights. So, we just…listened to music and talked about everything except whatever it was he wanted to ask me. Though he did ask a few other questions about my life in the trailer.

When we were coming around the bend that led down to the bridge, Craig said, "Okay, here's what I wanted to ask—you really saw divers in this river? Our river? Like, actual scuba divers?"

And I was like, "Yeah. They were boy scouts."

And then, Craig said, "Could you show me where?"

And of course, I said yes, so Craig parked in what was usually the lot for the train station, and then we walked over the grass and across the street and down the sidewalk to the bridge. It was my first time being on the bridge on foot since that one day with my dad. It was so late by then that the restaurant on the bank was on the verge of closing—there was no one left on the dining patio. They were still playing music, but all I could hear was "say you love me now," which is, like, the most generic song lyric ever, so I never found out exactly what song it was when I tried to look it up later.

You could still see the stars, even with the town lights. The river was so smooth it was like glass, and the moon was, like, reflecting off it. It only did that at certain hours—it had to rise over the mountain, which you could still see as an outline on a clear night.

So, I...walked Craig out to the middle of the bridge and pointed down, and then I said, "There—that's where we saw them coming up. They made a camp on that little island, and my dad took me down to meet them."

Craig nodded and said, "Sweet."

And I said, "I actually joined the boy scouts for a while— well, the cub scouts. My dad and I did it together. I just...wasn't interested in keeping it up past the cub scout level. It wasn't as adventurous as I thought it'd be."

And Craig just went, "Mmm."

So, then, I said, "I'm sorry, I know this must be more boring than you expected. It all happened a long time ago— there's nothing down there anymore. I don't even know what they found underwater. I don't remember them bringing anything up."

And then, Craig said, "This isn't boring. I'm not bored."

And I felt like I had to say, "I didn't really beg you to hang out with me, right?"

And Craig was like, "What? No. You're, like, the most fun kid I've ever met."

And I was like.... "Really?"

And he said, "Yeah! I told you my parents never let me play video games before I met you, and I never had anyone to stand outside with me, either—that was mostly about getting away from other kids who only, like, half knew what to do with me."

So, I said, "Well, I understand that." Because I did.

And then, he said, "Alan, do you know why I dress like this?" And he spread out his arms to show his outfit.

And I was like, "Uh…because you're a…punk?" Again, it had never directly come up before, for all my early wondering about it. It kind of just became a thing that…was, to me. I'd never even asked myself why someone would become a punk.

But Craig just laughed and said, "I'm not even sure I really count as that. But anyway, I started wearing the bracelets and the collars and the shiny pants to make my parents pay more attention to me. It was aggressive. But you made it mean something else, and I like it a lot better now because it got you to do all this stuff with me. Do you…I mean, do you see what I'm saying? This outfit was designed to push on people, but it pulled you in, and that's…I just…I hate the idea that Jack getting in your head about it could cause you to not see that, even for a second. It honestly just…it honestly makes me want to give you some kind of proof you can't ignore."

And I turned to look at the moon on the water again, because I was high-speed asking myself if he was really

saying what I thought he was saying, and while I was still
turned around like that, he kissed me. On the cheek.

And, I mean, I…like…I mean, like…I'd seen the rainbow
flag around town since I was little, and my mom told me
what it meant the first time I asked, so I knew what this was,
and I knew I was okay with it, but, like…I just never thought
it would happen. I didn't even have an image of it in my head,
or at least I thought I didn't, but maybe I just couldn't look at
it, like how I couldn't look at the computer screen when it
said I was "bizarre."

Anyway, I…after he kissed me, I turned back around, but
I only looked at him for, like, a second, because then I had to
get up on my tiptoes and kiss him, too, on the lips. And then,
I put my arms around him, and he put his arms around me,
and I heard him sucking in air through his nose, so I did that,
too, and then he put his tongue in my mouth, and I put my
tongue in his mouth, and then he, like, lifted his leg up in
between my legs and I was like hnnnnNNNNnnng. I didn't
even know I could make sounds like the ones I made that
night. It made Craig laugh once, and that made me laugh,
too, and after that, we were still kissing. Nothing I did
weirded him out. There was nothing left I couldn't share.

It was…awesome.

CHAPTER 11
RAVENFEATHER

Jack and I didn't talk for a while after that. I probably would've still gone back to the lunch table and just sat farther away from him—maybe tried to talk to Aloysius or something instead, so the next time I wound up at a party it wouldn't be so awkward—but everyone was starting to get their drivers' licenses by then, or they knew someone who did, so they were all going out to eat, and that included me. I usually just sat in the car with Craig in the parking lot, but technically, that was still going out.

I don't even think I wanted to talk to Jack. I felt like I'd outgrown him, and at the time, I thought, he obviously hated me anyway, so what was there left to say? It actually...jolted me the next time I ran into him, about a month after the start of junior year. He was taking out his family's garbage again, just like the time he caught me dressed as Grabberman, and I was about to walk past him on my way home from picking up some stuff at the deli for Nana, but I didn't notice him on the sidewalk until I got close—there was a bush in the way—so I just said a quick hi, and he said hi back, and I started to cut around him, but then he stopped me.

And he said, "No, Alan, wait. I'm sorry. There's something I have to say. And...well, I guess that's it, actually. I'm sorry."

And I said, "Sorry for what?" Because I genuinely wasn't sure at that point.

And Jack said, "For...taking you for granted, I guess. You're right—I really did put most of my energy into all our other friends. But, Alan, please, I need you to understand that that was just because I always knew you were the one friend who'd never abandon me. I didn't have to fight to keep you the way I did with everyone else. I feel like the second I'm not interesting, Honoria's gonna dump me, and Ben and Bram will find someone else to play cards with, and that'll be it, so I have to be, like, on all the time. I have to act perfectly cool and, like, always know what to say or what to tell the group to do. But, Alan, you were friends with me before anyone was cool. Remember those comics we used to draw, or how we used to play freaking Old Maid or Go Fish for hours on my back deck? I was never worried about losing you, but...I guess that means I also never felt like I had to do anything to keep you, and that wasn't fair, so...I'm sorry."

And at first, I was just, like, "Oh." I really had no idea Jack thought any of that. He always seemed so...confident and in control. I didn't know what to say.

Eventually, I did say, "So, you and Honoria are dating now?"

And Jack was like, "Heh, yeah. We made it official last month. If everything goes well, we'll probably end up going to prom together next spring." I hadn't even thought about prom. Then, Jack said, "There was a time when I might've asked to make sure you didn't mind, but...I guess I've known you wouldn't for a while now."

And I didn't say anything, because I really didn't want to get back on the subject of Craig or my...you know, with Jack. Once was enough.

And then, Jack said, "So, can we just go back to having game nights, then? I just got the Nintendo 64."

And I said, "Oh, awesome! I've only seen a demo of that in the store. I'd love to try it." Sometimes, I did go to the game store on my own by then, or with Craig. It helped me figure out what I wanted for my birthday, or Christmas—and let me just stop to say that I'm really lucky I had a family that was so generous and loving.

Anyway, Jack said, "Yeah, sure! Come over anytime. Bring your punk friend if you want."

And I said, "Yeah, maybe." But really, I didn't think I wanted to put Jack and Craig in the same room. I'd seen how Jack acted when it wasn't just the two of us, and hearing him describe it from his end really put it into perspective for me. He had a long way to go to prove that he was really gonna start prioritizing me more instead of making me a sacrifice for his popularity, and until then, being around him with Craig was…well, it wasn't safe.

Anyway, speaking of Craig…well, I mean, we kept having lunch together, and our schedules overlapped more once I was a junior and he was a senior, because seniors have more frees, and…we kept talking, and hanging out, and playing games, and…we kept kissing…and my mom invited him to come over for Thanksgiving, but he said no because he didn't want to disappoint his family—which I think really meant he was afraid they'd get mad at him if he didn't show—but he did come by after dinner and ask if I wanted to go to Berensdale Winterfest with him, and of course, I said yes. So, I ended up meeting him uptown on December 9th, just past Sulley's. Every store had stuff out on the sidewalk—most of it with heaters so the shop owners didn't freeze to death— and the old well at the town common had a bunch of lights on the metal...awning, over it, I guess is what it was called. The main event of the night was the lighting of the town Christmas tree, a little past the well, but it was all uphill, so you could see it from pretty much anywhere. Craig staked us out a spot to watch on the lawn of an old church that got turned into a concert venue when I was little. He waved to help me find him when I got there.

So, I walked up, and Craig said, "Hey."

And I said, "Hey. I like your jacket." Craig had one of those green army surplus jackets for winter—I guess I knew by then that his family was pretty poor. I tried not to wave all the stuff I had in his face when he came over.

And Craig...smiled up at me and said, "Are you sure? It's not shiny."

And I said, "No, I think it looks good on you." And I did.

When I sat down, Craig inched up one of the sleeves a little and said, "Don't worry, I've still got our friendship bracelet on." And I real-quick touched it, and then I real-quick kissed him.

We watched the tree lighting, and the whole town went "ooooo," and then we walked around for a while and went into some of the stores. Sulley's smelled like pine needles at that time of year. We got some roasted chestnuts after I smelled them cooking and said my granddad liked them, but when we tried them, I couldn't figure out why, because they were disgusting, and we wound up throwing the rest of them away.

But after we were done, Craig said, "Hey, would you mind walking home with me? I have to give you your Christmas present."

And I was like, "You bought me a Christmas present?! But I didn't get you anything!"

But before I could panic too much, he said, "Don't worry, I didn't actually 'buy' anything. I wouldn't have had the money to do it even if I wanted to. It's just...you'll see. Come on."

So, we walked up past the tree and out of downtown, went over the little bridge by a backwater of the river, and eventually, we came up to the supermarkets and restaurants Craig lived behind. At one point, we got hit with this incredibly cold wind and I started shivering—I really needed a new jacket at that point—but Craig saw and he linked arms with me for warmth, which was so sweet of him.

I'd only been over to Craig's house twice—he liked hanging out at my house better—but, like...what I mean is, I knew how to find his room without him having to guide me, which was good, because he went in first. When I caught up, he was still rooting around under his bed. He had this big poster on his wall from an old kid's magazine—it was a giant maze—so I tried to solve it with my finger while I waited for him to finish. Eventually, he came up with a plastic supermarket bag tied at the top, and he said, "Surprise!" And then, he handed it to me.

I honestly have no idea what face I must've made when I opened that bag, because inside it was The Pants. Or, rather, a pair of the same or very similar pants.

Craig said they were his old ones from before he got taller. He said, "I've actually been thinking about giving them to you since the first time I went over to your place. I knew you'd like them, and I had no use for them anymore, so why not? I actually, uh…I actually checked your pants size while you were in the bathroom that night, just to make sure they'd fit. Didn't want to get your hopes up if I wasn't sure."

And I said, "So, that's what you were doing!" It wasn't exactly what I thought, but…I actually think it was even better.

And then, Craig waved to me and was like, "Go ahead, try them on."

And I was like, "Okay, give me a little privacy, please." Because I was blushing my face off. And Craig laughed and turned around and covered his eyes while I took my khakis off and put his old pants on. And, like…they felt so much better than I even imagined they would. Soft on the inside, shiny on the outside. By the time I said "okay" to let Craig turn around and then "ta-da" to show off to him, my voice was really quiet, because I...couldn't really breathe.

And then, Craig said, "Here, let's be twins," and he took out his current pair of The Pants from under his mattress, at which point, it was my turn to look away. And then, when we were both dressed up, Craig opened his closet door so the mirror inside was facing us, and he put his arm around me and said, "I think we look pretty good, right?"

And I said, "Yeah," but it came out really airy because I was already going in to kiss him, and he put his leg between my legs again after he grabbed onto me, and it felt even better than last time because of how we were both dressed, and then I started raising my left leg like I...like I was climbing up on him, and then he spun me around and pushed me down backwards so I fell onto his bed, and...you know what, actually, I think I'll leave this part out. Suffice it to say that a half-hour later, when we started talking again, the only clothes still on us were those two pairs of pants.

So, Craig was like, "That was fun."

And I was like, "Yeah." And then, he kissed me again, on the lips, and then he started kissing me down my chest and actually, I think I'll leave this part out a bit, too.

But eventually, he said, "I love what this stuff does to you."

And I was like, "What do you mean?"

And he said, "I mean it makes you, like, a hundred times more confident. Or…no, that's not it. It makes you more assertive. You're always the one who kisses me first when I'm dressed up for it. It's like you want it so bad it overrides your wholesomeness."

And, like…I knew he was right as soon as he said it, so I said, "Yeah, I guess it does." But this was like a revelation to me.

And then, Craig was like, "You know what else would be fun?" And he put on this really impy smile.

And I asked, "What?"

And then, he stood up and grabbed my sweater, and tossed it down to me, and said, "If you got to show off your new outfit around town."

And I was like, "What?!" And I covered my pants with my sweater as if anyone besides Craig could see me right then— it was a good thing he'd told me his parents weren't in the house that night—and I said, "I can't walk around town like this! Everyone would see me! Everyone would know."

And I was scared at first that I was gonna hurt Craig by pushing him off, but then he, like, slapped his forehead and said, "Duh, I'm dumb. Of course you can't. For me, dressing up like this is about getting a reaction—or at least it was—but for you, walking around in those pants would be like walking around with no pants at all, right? Of course you wouldn't want random people to see you naked. I'm glad I'm not random anymore, though."

And that—THAT—was my lightning bulb moment. Lightning bolt? Light bulb? Either way, that was the moment I really got it, because Craig got it—he got it for me. That was why the things I liked, or...the things that interested me always felt like secrets, and why I always got nervous whenever someone else came too close to seeing them. It's not that I was embarrassed—it was never about embarrassment. It really was just like being naked—it was my sexuality. Or I guess it...became that. That was why I had to keep my collection away from my family, even though I knew they'd never stop loving me or anything. That was the boundary Jack crossed without permission. All of what I've told you, all of what I grew up liking or being...drawn in by was actually tied into the development of a part of myself that's really great, but also...really private. And, like, that's okay. I realized with Craig, then, that it's okay to have that kind of a boundary. It's okay to decide how and when you like the stuff you like and who you let in to see it.

But then Craig was like, "You know what, though? Maybe the problem is that the people around here aren't random enough. Would you be willing to try something with me?"

And I said, "Sure, okay. I trust you."

And then, Craig smiled in another way I'd never seen him smile before and said, "Great. Put your regular pants on over those pants and come on."

So, what Craig did was drive us down to Ferrisburg. He said that was as good a time as any to change me never having been there, and he also said he had something else to show me there, so I was curious. I actually ended up being glad I wore two pairs of pants for that trip, because the heat in Craig's mom's car was never that good, and it got drafty on the highway. Besides, it felt kind of exciting to have my secret so close to the surface and yet still so hidden. Craig didn't put anything on over his pants, but like he said, it wasn't exactly the same thing for him.

It was only about a forty minute drive, though it…did take us an extra fifteen minutes to find parking. After we parked, though, Craig took me around the block and said "ta-da," and if it had been anyone else, I would've thought he was making fun of me, but it was really more just like he was taking his turn. It took me a second, but I realized I was looking at Pointed Question—the store Craig told me about where he bought our "friendship bracelet."

And for a second, my, like, heart pounded, because I was carrying enough money to buy one for myself, but then Craig was like, "Oh. It's closed. Wait, of course it is, what was I thinking? It's, like, 9:00 on a Saturday."

And I said, "It's okay. We can come back."

And then, Craig said, "Sure, but this is only part of what I wanted to show you anyway. Come on, take a walk with me."

So, I did. And I realized that just because Pointed Question was closed didn't mean everything was—the whole street was crawling with people. And I realized that most of the couples there were either two men or two women. And mostly also much older than us, but, like, a lot of them were wearing leather jackets, and a lot of the women were wearing fishnet stockings, and a lot of the stores were clothing stores with black mannequins that had, like…belt buckles over their chests—I still don't understand that—but the point was, nobody was looking twice at Craig's pants. Some of them were nodding at him in a friendly way, sure, but it was like…this was routine here, in Ferrisburg, or at least in this part of Ferrisburg. And not a single one of those people was someone I knew. We were just far enough from home that there was virtually no chance of running into anyone from school, and I knew my family almost never drove down that way.

Then, Craig said, "So, this is the Ravenfeather section of Ferrisburg. I used to come here all the time, even when I had to take the train. It's the one place where no one ever tried to make me be someone I wasn't."

And I was like, "Yeah, I can see that."

And then, we passed an alley behind what I think was a restaurant, and Craig, like, tilted his head that way and said, "I used to pee back there. You can probably change behind the dumpster…if you want to, that is. I can carry your pants for you. Your…other pants."

And you know what? I said, "Okay!" And I was really excited! My hands were shaking when I undressed down to the pants Craig had just given me, but it wasn't out of fear. Well, it might've been a tiny bit out of fear, and probably also a little out of the cold—Craig's pants, or, my pants, I should say, weren't as insulated as my regular pants. But I didn't care. When I came back out, Craig did take my khakis, but he also wanted to hold hands, and I…wanted to hold hands, too. It helped keep me warm.

So, we just walked around Ravenfeather like that for about half an hour. I saw every store and restaurant and bar I wasn't old enough to go into yet, and they were all full of people who I just…knew wouldn't judge me. Couldn't judge me. How could they? They were just like me.

At one point, this lady we walked past, who had a surprisingly deep voice, said to the other lady with her, "Aww, look at how cute."

And after they were gone, Craig said, "Well, she's right about that." And then, he kissed me on the cheek again. And it was nice. It was just…it was just really nice.

About the Author

Jonathan V. Cann was born in Manhattan, raised in New Jersey, and educated in upstate New York. Currently a resident of Queens—one of the ancestral homes of his family—he works during the day as a systems administrator and mentor to the next generation of writers and thinkers, while spending as much time as possible writing and curating novels, video games, and comics for small and very specific audiences. He never plans to stop making things.